"You look shattered, Miss Williams. Why?"

"I am," Lee gasped. "You don't ... you can't ask someone you've just met to be your wife! Marriage isn't a business arrangement."

"For me it is," he said. "You arrived here expecting to be married, but the man you expected to marry has gone. I, on the other hand, have to marry before the end of this week. I suggest we amalgamate. I'm asking you to marry me."

His cool approach repelled and fascinated her at the same time. "There must be other women you could ask," she said, guessing instinctively that no man as attractive and as wealthy as Max Van Breedan would be without friends.

"There are," he replied dryly. "But none are nice, young and innocent like you!"

OTHER
Harlequin Romances
by FLORA KIDD

Many of these titles are available at your local bookseller
or through the Harlequin Reader Service.

For a free catalogue listing all available Harlequin Romances,
send your name and address to:

HARLEQUIN READER SERVICE,
M.P.O. Box 707, Niagara Falls, N.Y. 14302
Canadian address: Stratford, Ontario, Canada N5A 6W2

or use coupon at back of book.

The Bargain Bride

by

FLORA KIDD

Harlequin Books

TORONTO • LONDON • NEW YORK • AMSTERDAM
SYDNEY • HAMBURG • PARIS

Original hardcover edition published in 1976
by Mills & Boon Limited

ISBN 0-373-02228-X

Harlequin edition published January 1979

Printed in Canada

CHAPTER ONE

LEE stepped down the wooden steps of the shabby house which advertised itself as a private hotel. Although it was only ten o'clock on a morning in late January the rays of the sun were bright and white-hot as they shone down mercilessly on to Curaçao, one of the Dutch Leewards, which are flung like stones of amber into the turquoise setting of the Caribbean Sea, close to the northern coast of South America.

The road was dusty. It was edged by houses which were painted various pastel shades now faded by the onslaught of the sun. No trees grew there to cast shade, but a few cacti struggled to survive by the wayside.

She reached a drawbridge which spanned a narrow canal-like inlet of water, a glittering reflection of the sky. On the other side of the bridge was the Punda, the fashionable shopping district of Willemstad, and it was among the cluster of tile-roofed buildings she could see there that Lee hoped to find Adrian.

The thought of meeting again the young man she had come here to marry made her step out hopefully. She walked gracefully, as if to the sound of music. A gust of wind swept down the inlet and tweaked cheekily at the skirt of her sun-dress, lifting the flounce which edged it, belling the skirt out and up to reveal her shapely legs.

As she tried to hold the skirt down the wind snatched at the brim of her sun-hat, threatening to lift it from her head, and for a moment she was in difficulties as she tried to hold the hat on with one hand and the skirt down with the other. Her problem caught the admiring attention of some young

5

working men who were riding by in the back of a truck. They whistled at her, as young men anywhere will whistle at a young woman who finds herself in similar difficulties.

Smiling a little at the whistling, Lee reached the end of the bridge and paused to get her bearings as she recalled the instructions given to her at the hotel. Then, seeing the silhouettes of short masts and the squat shapes of sturdy boats crowding along the edge of a solid stone wharf, she recognised the floating market which had been described to her, so she turned right to walk along the wide street which flanked the narrow inlet.

When she was close to the boats she slowed down to gaze at the long rows of brown-flecked pale yellow bananas and the pyramids of emerald green peppers; at the piles of scarlet tomatoes spilling over among limes, lemons and oranges and the golden sheen of onions. They were all spread out with fish and other foods, under makeshift awnings of sails and flour bags hung out from the rigging of the boats.

Tilting her head to one side, Lee read the writing on one of the flour bags. It was in Spanish and, as she lingered, she caught the lilt of the same language as a tawny-skinned Curaçaon housewife wearing a bright pink cotton dress, her hair covered by a kerchief of the same colour, bargained with a swarthy Venezuelan vendor who only that morning had brought his produce to market in the sturdy sloop which was tied up behind him.

Resisting the temptation to buy some fruit, knowing she must be careful how she spent her small amount of money, Lee moved away and was immediately struck by the contrast offered by the neat row of buildings she was passing with the sloops and schooners of the floating market.

Some of the buildings were tall and narrow with high sloping roofs of reddish-brown tiles. Others were broad and bland and had curved rococo gables decorated with painted whorls and scrolls. Some buildings had broad columns supporting the upper storeys over cool shadowy arcades, others had rows of long galleries running along their façades. Some had small, secretive windows, while others had wide smiling ones curving under elegant arches.

But all the buildings looked as if they had been lifted intact from Holland and placed beside the glittering inlet of the sea, and all were an expression of the spirit of the people who had colonised the island; that mixture of solidity and jollity characteristic of the Dutch burghers. There was a difference though. Instead of being the colour of sturdy red brick, like the buildings she had known in Amsterdam where Lee had been living until recently, they were painted pretty eye-soothing colours: lavender, rose, lime, olive and amber.

Pleased by what she could see—because it was familiar, and familiarity brought with it a sense of security to her in that tropical island, so far from the cool winds and cool colours of north-west Europe—Lee turned along a street which delved into the town. She was searching for a name and soon she saw it, printed in white above an arched doorway in a building which looked just like a gingerbread house decorated with white icing, straight out of a fairy tale.

Outside the main entrance to the shop she hesitated and nibbled at her lower lip, suddenly nervous. Then she caught sight of her reflection in a plate glass window. Disliking the slump of her slim shoulders and the way her shoulder blades were poking through the skin of her back, left bare by her sun-dress, she straightened up, lifted her chin and swung with unconscious grace through the open door of the shop.

Inside was cool and hushed, almost like a place of worship. Smartly-dressed women attended by smartly-dressed men hovered over long glass showcases, which were set about a floor covered by thick-piled carpet the colour of

7

golden toast.

A little awed by the tasteful decorations of the place, Lee moved slowly, almost reverently, among the showcases. At one customers were examining and comparing the fine golden jewellery which was on display. At another they were selecting fine linens from Madeira and Ireland. At yet another Delft china, hand-painted and blue, was being admired along with Hummel figurines.

Lee's quick ears caught the sound of English being spoken, and she went over to a counter to wait until the customer who was being served had gone. Then she asked the assistant to direct her to the personnel office of the company.

The lift she took was smooth, swift and silent. Its doors slid open and she stepped into a wide sunlit passage. A sign above a doorway said Information in several different languages, and beside the door was a window of frosted glass which was open. Through it she could see several women working at desks. She tapped on the glass and the nearest woman looked up and came to the window.

'Can I help you?' she asked in English, and Lee's golden-brown eyes went wide.

'How did you know which language to use?' she asked.

'After a while one becomes accustomed to distinguishing one nationality from another,' said the woman with a smile. 'To me you look very English and your clothes are English. What can I do for you?'

'I'm looking for Adrian Hartog. He works here,' said Lee.

The woman frowned as if trying to recall if she knew anyone of that name, shook her head and said,

'One moment, please.'

She turned away and went to her desk, picked up the telephone receiver. Her finger flicked the dial several times and as she waited for an answer she glanced back at Lee, still

8

frowning.

He's got to be here. He must be here, Lee said over and over to herself. When she had arrived the day before at the airport after a long tedious flight from Amsterdam, the hopes raised by her impulsive decision to fly out to Curaçao and join Adrian had given way to a desperate fear that perhaps she had acted too impulsively, because although she had sent a cable to him asking him to meet her, he had not been in the arrival lounge to greet her.

After waiting to see if he would come she had at last given up, had found out the name and whereabouts of a good but cheap hotel, and had gone to it by taxi. From the hotel she had phoned the Van Breedan Company offices, but they had been closed for the night. Since Adrian had always used a Post Office box number as his address she had no idea where he lived, so she had decided to wait until morning to call at the company in person to find him.

The woman was talking rapidly into the phone in Dutch, then was silent as she listened to the person on the other end of the line. Eventually she laid down the receiver on the desk and came across to Lee.

'Your name, please?' she asked.

'Lee Williams.'

The woman went back to the telephone and after a further brief conversation she replaced the receiver and came back to the window. Her bland solid-looking face gave nothing away. Whatever she had learned about the whereabouts of Adrian Hartog was not to be passed on.

'You are to go to see the boss,' she said, giving the last word the usual Dutch pronunciation of *baas*. 'Go to your right along the corridor, to the door at the end. You will find his secretary there. She will direct you further. Good morning.'

'Thank you. Good morning.'

The boss. Who could that be? Vincent Van Breedan, of

9

course, Adrian's father's friend who had found Adrian a place in his company and was training him in the business. Yes, the boss was sure to know where Adrian was because for a while he had been Adrian's guardian and he was interested in the welfare of his friend's son.

Lee's spirits lifted again. Everything was going to be all right after all! The fears and suspicions which had made her restless the previous night had been unfounded. In a few minutes she would know where Adrian was, perhaps even be greeted by him.

She knocked on the door at the end of the corridor and gazed at the sign which was printed on it. Vincent Van Breedan was the president of the company, a family enterprise which had been going since the eighteenth century, when the first Van Breedan had brought in goods from Europe to trade, not only with the colonists on the islands, but also with the neighbouring South American countries.

A voice told her to enter and she went into a big room which was shaded by venetian blinds from the bright rays of the sun. Two women were in the room; a small coal-black girl with fuzzy hair was tapping away at a typewriter at a small desk, while behind another larger desk sat an older woman whose sleek black hair was wound in a chignon round her small head. She was writing something on a pad of paper, but as Lee approached the desk she looked up, and her big dark eyes widened slightly as they surveyed in turn Lee's white hat, from under which her thick, slightly wavy auburn hair hung in a shining mass; the creamy complexion of her fine-featured face, and the stark simplicity of her green cotton sun-dress with its pinafore bodice and cross-over straps.

'You are Miss Williams?' she asked, speaking English with a lovely lilting accent.

'Yes,' Lee agreed.

'I am Cora de Palm.' The woman smiled, her thick lips

parting over big white teeth. 'I'm Mr Van Breedan's secretary. He is on the phone right now, but he said I could send you in as soon as you came. This way.'

Lee followed the elegantly swaying hips of Cora de Palm through another door into a room which was also shaded by venetian blinds. The door closed behind her and she stood hesitantly, looking at the man behind the desk set in front of the windows.

He was leaning back in a leather-covered swivel chair and his well-shod feet were resting on the corner of the desk. He was talking into the telephone receiver in a strange language which sounded like a record of someone speaking being played backwards at the wrong speed. It sounded to Lee like a mixture of Dutch, Spanish and Portuguese, with several words of English thrown in together with many other unintelligible words.

Having always been fascinated by language she went forward slowly, listening intently to the deep voice. The man did not seem to realise she was there, because he continued to talk into the phone without looking up. Soon she was standing in front of him and she could see that he had a blunt-featured, square-jawed face, the skin olive-tinted, and that his curling hair, his eyebrows and thick sideburns were a luxuriant raven black.

Solid Dutch worth sheathed in a cloak of South American leather.

Lee was surprised at her own flight of fancy. Yet the mixture would not be unusual here in this island, where people from many different lands and origins had met and mingled for hundreds of years. He was wearing a crisp black cotton shirt and light grey trousers. His casual attitude—feet on the corner of the desk, unbuttoned shirt collar, loosened silk tie and rolled-up shirt-sleeves—hinted at an influence which was not Dutch, and showed a dislike of formality which was not in keeping with his presence in

11

the presidential chair of the company.

He looked up at her suddenly and shock quivered through her, for his eyes were light grey, steel-bright between thick black lashes, like the glittering points of two daggers seen in a room dark with shadow. Raising his free hand, in which he held a half-smoked cigar, he pointed with a blunt forefinger at the chair on her side of the desk. After a slight hesitation she sat down on the edge of the chair and removed her hat, which was making her feel hot.

Sitting upright, unaware that stray shafts of sunlight filtering through the slats of the blinds, were highlighting her hair and making it blaze here and there with copper sparks, Lee continued to watch the man behind the desk, absolutely fascinated by the enigma which his physical appearance presented.

He was listening now, occasionally giving a grunt to show he was interested in what the person at the other end of the line was saying. His eyes were hidden again but, as he lifted the cigar to his mouth to puff at it, he gave her another quick penetrating glance and again she felt herself quiver in reaction.

He wasn't the sort of person she had expected Vincent Van Breedan to be. She had pictured a man in his late fifties, worldly-wise but kindly. The man lounging there so insolently was in his mid-thirties, she guessed; he looked worldly, but not at all kind. A person whose glance stabbed right through you as his did, whose mouth lifted in an ironic twist, whose deep voice had a hard icy edge to it when he interrupted the other speaker with some rapid words, could not possibly be described as kindly.

His eyes lifted to her again and this time their glance lingered. Lee looked away sharply, lifting her chin, and glanced round the room. Some pictures of sailing boats on a nearby wall caught her attention—they were dinghies racing, sails taut and shining, bows thrusting through the water, making spray fly. Beside the pictures was a glass-fronted cupboard containing various cups and tankards, obviously trophies won in some sport. Her glance passed on, noting books in several languages in a bookcase which was topped by a beautiful model of a sailing ship, complete with squaresails and topsails.

Slowly her glance came back to the desk which was being desecrated by Van Breedan's feet. It was a noble antique, made from dark wood and intricately carved; it looked Spanish, possibly a piece of loot stolen from a Spanish treasure ship by some Dutch pirate long ago. And, as if prompted by that thought, her glance lifted again to the tough swarthy face of the man behind the desk. Never had she seen anyone better suited to be cast in the role of a buccaneer!

He laughed suddenly at something which was being said to him. The sound wasn't kind. It wasn't jolly either. It was satirical and it changed his face, taking away the impression of stolidity and giving it an attractive devilry which made her want to run from the room. His lips curved back over even white teeth and Lee averted her gaze quickly.

'What do you want with Adrian Hartog?'

The brusque question spoken in fluent, accentless English made her jump. While she had been day-dreaming he had finished his phone call, swung his feet down from the desk and was now leaning forward both elbows on the desk as he took another pull at his cigar.

'I would like to see him, please,' she replied, hoping she appeared poised and self-confident, although his abrupt approach with its lack of the usual courtesies had put her off balance.

'Why?' he rapped.

'I ... he ... we ... didn't he tell you about me?' she asked defensively.

'Now why should he tell me about you?' he countered with a quirk of humour.

'Well, you're his guardian, and I thought . . .'

'His what?' Surprise sharpened his voice as he interrupted her.

'His guardian—at least you were once, and you've always taken an interest in his welfare. That's why you invited him to come out here to join the company and learn the business. He told me all about your friendship with his father and how good you've been to him.'

'Did he?' The touch of irony in his voice made her send a searching glance in his direction, but it was impossible for her to read the expression on his face because he had leaned back in his chair, and the smoke from the cigar made a convenient hazy screen. 'Where did you meet him?' he asked.

'In Amsterdam, last summer.'

'Were you on holiday there?'

'No, I was singing.' He turned his head to look sharply at her. The smoke haze had drifted away and she could see now that he was puzzled by her answer, so she hurried to explain, 'I was with a group singing at the Holland Festival. We sang folk-songs from different nations.'

'Unaccompanied?' His puzzlement had been replaced by interest, which had the effect of robbing his eyes of their steeliness, turning them the colour of the cigar-smoke.

'Oh, no.' Lee smiled so that her soft pink lips curved upwards at the corners, denting her cheeks with dimples. She felt more at ease now, warmed and disarmed by his interest. 'With guitar, lute and flute accompaniment. I play the guitar. I studied at a college of music in England before going to the Conservatory in Amsterdam.'

'You seem to be talented,' he remarked. 'Did you sing the songs in English or in Dutch?'

'Always in the original language. I sang the English songs

14

and some Spanish, Portuguese and Latin-American songs. Willi ... that is Willi Maarten, the leader of the group ... and his wife Greta sang the Dutch and Scandinavian songs. I met them when I was at the Conservatory, and with two other musicians we decided to make music together.'

'Were you successful at the Festival?' Van Breedan asked.

'We think we were, because we were hired afterwards for six months to sing at a club called the Golden Tulip. The contract expired at the end of December,' Lee explained.

'And you weren't re-hired?'

'Yes, we were, only I didn't want to stay because I wanted to come here, so a replacement was found for me.'

'Presumably you met Adrian at the club?' he inquired.

'Yes, he used to come every night last summer. He'd just finished studying at the university and was looking for a job. When the performance was over he used to come and talk to us.'

Lee's voice wavered to a stop and her face took on a wistful expression as memory winged back to those summer nights when she had lingered beside the Heerengracht in Amsterdam, under the elms beside the gabled red-brick mansions, watching reflections of light quivering in the water. Walking with Adrian, hearing him talking about the future—their future—feeling his kisses and his hands, rough and urgent, as he had pleaded with her.

'You must know Adrian is interested in music and poetry,' she added, shaking off the memory.

'No, I know nothing of his interests.' The deep voice was dry. 'I suppose you fell in love with him?'

'Yes, we fell in love,' she replied simply, looking straight at him.

'He too?' Now he was sceptical.

'Yes, that's why I'm here. We're going to be married,'

15

replied Lee, refusing to be put off by his attitude. It was quite obvious to her that he was a cynic about such things as love.

The silence which followed her statement seemed unduly heavy and ominous. Still sitting on the edge of the chair she watched motes of dust dance slowly in the shafts of sunlight slicing through the blinds.

The man leaned forward and ground out the remains of his cigar in an ashtray made of Scandinavian glass. His square face was impassive, giving away nothing of his thoughts as he continued with his inquisition.

'When did you last hear from Adrian?' he asked.

'Before Christmas. He isn't very good at writing,' she defended quickly.

'When he wrote did he invite you to come out here?'

'No. He didn't have to invite me. It was all arranged last September, before he left Amsterdam. He said it would be best if he came here alone, got settled in, and started to earn some money before we were married. I agreed because I was still under contract with the group and couldn't leave them.'

'Did you write to tell him you were coming?' he demanded.

'Yes, at the beginning of January.'

'Did he reply?'

'No. Unless. . .' His dagger-bright eyes glinted as she paused and bit her lip.

'Unless what?' he prompted.

'Unless his reply to my letter arrived after I left Amsterdam,' she faltered.

'I see. So you came here without knowing whether you would be welcome. Wasn't that a little reckless of you?' he persisted coolly.

Lee had been trying hard not to let his questioning irritate her, but she was not of the most equable temperament and now irritation simmered and boiled over. Eyes blazing with golden fire in her pale face, she retorted:

'Oh, I can see you're one of those cold-blooded people who make fun of love! Love doesn't wait to be invited. It goes where it's needed without being asked. Adrian didn't have to invite me to come and join him. He knew I'd come once I was free.'

'Whether he needed you or not.'

The words were spoken quietly, but they slashed through her as a knife slashes through skin and flesh in its search for the heart. Lee's heart seemed to stop temporarily as she caught her breath. Eyes wide, not with anger any more but with bewilderment, she sat silent as the awful fear she had experienced the previous night returned to nag her. Supposing Adrian had let her down? Supposing he had gone, what would she do?

'Did Adrian ever propose marriage to you?' The question stabbed into the wound which had just been inflicted. 'I notice you're not wearing an engagement ring, so I assume there was no formal announcement,' he went on relentlessly.

'No, there wasn't,' she admitted in a low voice. 'He . . . you see. . .' Her cheeks burned hot. 'It just happened,' she finished lamely. 'We decided to get married.'

'And soon after that decision was made he remembered he had a guardian and a job in Curaçao,' he murmured, one corner of his mouth curving downwards unpleasantly.

'Yes, he said it was the opportunity he had been waiting for.'

'I'm sure it was! An opportunity to escape from a commitment he wished he'd never made to you,' he suggested.

More fire sparked in Lee's eyes as she took exception to his remark. But it wouldn't do for her to antagonise her inquisitor by flaring out at him again. After all, he was the boss, and he held Adrian's future career in his large capable-looking hands, so she must try to keep the lid on her temper.

Taking a deep, unsteady breath, she said as calmly as she could:

'Mr Van Breedan, I came here to-day to find Adrian. I cabled him asking him to meet me at the airport yesterday, but he didn't turn up. I've no idea where he lives because he always used a Post Office box number or the company's address. Please will you tell me where I can find him?'

He was silent, his eyes veiled by their thick black lashes, his lower lip jutting pensively below the long curving upper lip. It was obvious he was considering her request seriously. Then he looked up in that sudden way he had, as if he hoped to surprise her doing something she shouldn't be doing.

'Before I tell you what has happened I have to clear up a little misunderstanding on your part,' he said. 'I am not Adrian's guardian and I never have been.'

'But aren't you Vincent Van Breedan?' she queried anxiously, afraid that she might have told all her secrets to an imposter.

'No. Vincent Van Breedan is my father. He retired from the presidency of the company a few years ago, because of ill health. I am Max Van Breedan, his younger son—I took over the management of the company when my elder brother Bruno was killed in an accident last October. Amongst several other awkward items and mistakes which he had collected during the course of his life, he bequeathed to me this Adrian Hartog, who had been given a position in the company on the strength of his father, Jan Hartog, having once been a close friend and associate of my father.' The deep voice crisped icily: 'At least that was the story Adrian told Bruno, and it worked. Bruno fell for that easy, fair-haired, blue-eyed charm no less than you did, Miss Williams. He took Adrian under his wing and gave him a job. But I must make it clear that he did not have to! My father was never Adrian's guardian and was under no obli-

18

gation to do anything for the son of Jan Hartog!'

Lee's skin felt clammy as a chill swept over her.

'You're saying that Adrian lied to me,' she accused shakily.

'I am,' he agreed grimly. 'Not only to you but to many other people too. That's why I had to kick him out.'

'Kick him out?' she repeated dully, and raised a hand to push back the fringe of her hair, which felt strangely wet and heavy against her forehead.

'Sack him, fire him, get rid of him, whichever expression you prefer,' he said bluntly. 'He left the company just before Christmas.'

A dark cloud seemed to be hovering in front of Lee's eyes, making it difficult for her to see. Frantically she blinked, hoping it would go away.

'Could you tell me where he's working now?' she asked.

'No, I couldn't,' he replied coldly.

'Then perhaps you could tell me where he lives,' she persisted.

'I'm not even sure he's on the island,' he returned thoughtfully.

The dark cloud descended slowly again and the room seemed to spin. Calling on all her resources, Lee clutched hold of her handbag in an endeavour to stay upright in the chair. She was aware of movement and looked up to see Max Von Breedan standing in front of her, his eyes bright and intent as he stared at her.

'Are you all right?' he asked laconically.

'Yes, thank you.' How faint and weak her voice sounded, and she seemed to have developed double vision because there were two of him. 'I'll be on my way now.' She stood up shakily, turning to go to the door, but he side-stepped neatly and blocked her way. She found herself looking at the loosened knot of his tie. It was made of grey silk and had a pattern of red squiggles on it.

'Sit down.' The terse order dispersed the black cloud which was clogging her mind and she tried to pull herself together.

'I really should go. You're busy,' she mumbled.

'I said sit down,' he rapped, and stepped towards her. He placed one large hand against her shoulder and pushed. She sat down with a jolt on the chair, and the shock suddenly roused her spirits. Flinging her hair back behind her shoulders, she glared up at him, intending to retort, but found her attention was sidetracked by his nearness.

He was taller than she had thought, his shoulders and chest broad and heavy under the taut black shirt, and the long thick muscles of his legs made hard shapes under the thin grey stuff of his trousers. He looked solid and reliable as he stood there watching her, the sort of person who could take responsibility and make decisions—who could inherit the awkward items collected by a brother and get rid of them. As he had got rid of Adrian.

'When did you eat last?' he asked, and the sharpness of his voice alerted her. The inquisition was beginning again.

'This morning,' she lied. She hadn't eaten because food was not provided at the hotel. In fact she had been shocked to discover that payment for the room in which she had slept did not include either breakfast or an evening meal.

'Are you sure it wasn't on the plane coming over yesterday?' he guessed shrewdly, and to her mortification her glance wavered and fell before his. Colour rushed into her cheeks, betraying the truth.

He swore softly and succinctly in Dutch and she glanced at him in alarm.

'How much money do you have with you?' was the next question, so quickly that she never thought to tell him it was none of his business how much money she had, but mumbled the amount. Again he swore savagely and quite unnecessarily, she thought.

'I've met some foolish people in my time, but you take first prize,' he grated exasperatedly. 'You've flown out here, using all your savings, I've no doubt, to buy a one-way ticket. You've been so caught up in a romantic spell of your own weaving that you've never considered that anything could go wrong. You've never looked beyond the moment of seeing Hartog waiting at the airport, ready to take you in his arms and kiss you welcome.'

His voice thickened with disgust and he broke off. Folding his arms across his chest, he stood with his head tipped forward and looked at her from under frowning brows as if waiting for an answer. But Lee had no answer ready. She was too crushed by his knowledgeable guesswork. Hers had been a one-way ticket to love and marriage, or so she had hoped.

'This is for real, Miss Williams,' he went on remorselessly, 'this is life as it happens all too often. Hartog has let you down and I'd even go so far as to say he probably didn't want to marry you or any other woman. He was just out for some fun. But you're the old-fashioned kind, you wouldn't play without marriage. So he agreed to marry you, then finding himself trapped, he ran away from Amsterdam, as far as he could get. Surely you don't want to find him now?'

'Yes, I do,' she muttered between teeth.

'But supposing you don't find him? Supposing he's left the island, what will you do then? You can't return to Europe because you haven't enough money for the fare. Perhaps you'll come back to me and expect me to pay for your ticket. I suspect you'll hold me responsible for his departure, if you can't find him,' he scoffed.

'Yes, I will, and I'm holding you responsible already! If it weren't for you Adrian would be here now,' she blazed. 'But I expect nothing from you. And even if you offered to pay for my return ticket I wouldn't accept. Accepting anything from you would be like accepting a gift from the devil—I'm sure you'd want something in return.'

His crack of laughter surprised and warned her at the same time. It warned her that she would get nowhere by flinging insults at him; he was too hard to feel them.

'You're quite right, I would want something in return. I'm as thrifty as the next Dutchman and I only lend money when I'm sure it's going to earn interest at a good rate.' He paused, then added slowly and suggestively, 'I *give* it in return for favours granted to me, or for a job well done.'

He eyed her with slow speculation, so that she felt like a piece of merchandise he was appraising before deciding to purchase it.

'You're a pretty young thing,' he drawled, and she flinched in reaction to the careless compliment which seemed to be deliberately designed to put her in her place as an object which could be bought or sold. All her innate independence rose up to do battle, but before she could speak he leaned forward and touched one of her cheekbones with a forefinger. Slowly the fingertip slid down to trace the hollow of her cheek and to trail along the fine angle of her jawbone.

It was a strange, impersonal caress which sent a shudder through her body. So might he have touched a fine piece of Delft china, or caressed the lines of an elegant crystal goblet to test its value.

'A young woman like you should have soft curves and a bloom on her cheeks. You've been starving yourself. Was it for love or for music?' he scoffed softly, standing away from her and thrusting his hands in his trouser pockets. Eyes half closed, he continued to appraise her. 'How long is it since there was anyone to look after you, to see that you eat properly, go to bed early and to stop you from giving in to foolish romantic impulses which land you in foreign countries without enough money?'

'I don't need anyone to look after me,' she retorted spiritedly. 'I've been looking after myself for four years, ever since I was eighteen.'

'That makes you twenty-two. You look younger, but that's because you're too thin. What happened? Did you leave home of your own accord or were you thrown out?'

'Oh!' she gasped, outraged by this insinuation. 'I wasn't thrown out of anywhere. My mother died when I was twelve. After that, when I wasn't at boarding school, I lived with my father. He was a musician too, and played the trumpet in an orchestra. Just before my eighteenth birthday he was killed when the orchestra bus collided with another vehicle on its return from a concert tour of the North of England. I was able to continue my education because he left sufficient money in trust for me to do that. Does that answer your question?'

'Admirably,' he drawled, and she saw mockery flicker elusively in his eyes.

'Then I'll go now,' she said determinedly. Slinging the strap of her handbag over one shoulder, she stood up. 'Thank you for taking the trouble to tell me about Adrian personally. I'm sure it's given you a great deal of pleasure,' she added rather acidly.

'It has, but not in the way you think,' he murmured enigmatically. 'Where are you going now?'

'To look for Adrian. You see, I don't believe a word you've said about him,' she retorted.

'So you're one of those women who has to see for yourself before you take the word of a stranger?' he remarked. 'That's an awful lot of faith and tenacity to waste on a weak-kneed scrounger like Hartog.' As she opened her mouth to protest against his description of Adrian, he said quickly, 'All right, I know you don't think he's a scrounger. I'll make it a little easier for you by giving you the address of the last place he lived in. He might be there—or the owners of the house might know where he has gone.'

She followed him through the door into the outer office.

'Cora, give Miss Williams Adrian Hartog's last address will you please?' The deep voice was brisk, businesslike. 'I expect Personnel have it in their files.'

'*Ja, meneer.*'

'Good morning, Miss Williams.' There was no softening of the voice and the grey eyes were blank, utterly impersonal.

'Goodbye, Mr Van Breedan,' she returned coolly. 'Thank you for your help,' she added a little diffidently, thinking she should at least appear polite in front of the secretary and typist, but he had turned away and was going through the door into his office. The door closed with a click of finality, giving the impression that he was glad to close it on the problem of Lee Williams in search of Adrian Hartog.

Cora de Palm directed her to be seated and she sat down thankfully while the secretary contacted the personnel department and then, taking a sheet of paper bearing the company's name and address, wrote some words on it.

'There you are, Miss Williams,' she said, handing the sheet of paper across the desk.

Lee thanked her and looked down at the name of the street written there.

'Is it far from here?' she asked.

'No, you can walk there. It is near Berg Altena Street. If you ask anyone outside they will direct you to it. It is a very old street where the slaves used to live; this other street crosses it at the top. If you'd like to wait until twelve o'clock, I will go with you.'

The dark eyes were surveying her anxiously and she wondered if she looked paler than usual. Certainly her head was behaving in a most peculiar way.

'No, thank you. That's very kind of you, but I'll find it all right. Goodbye.'

24

She made it through the door into the corridor, but once there she leaned against the wall for a moment, waiting for the tilting of the floor and the swaying of the walls to stop. After a few minutes everything seemed to be back to normal, so she walked to the elevator which took her in one smooth swoop to the ground floor. Again she wended her way through the showcases and the well-dressed tourists, who were buying, and went towards the bright sunlight of the street.

Heat hit her like a blow, and she put her hand to her head. No hat! She must have left it in the office of that detestable man, and nothing would make her return for it. She wasn't going to face again the dagger-sharp glint of those hard grey eyes which seemed to pierce through to her very soul. She wasn't going to listen to his criticism of her impulsive behaviour all over again. In fact she never wanted to see Max Van Breedan again in her life!

Berg Altena Street tilted steeply up a hillside, small terraced houses rising one above the other like steps. They had narrow double doors and two narrow windows. The stops of the doors and the wooden shutters covering the windows were slatted to allow air to get in but to keep bright sunlight out. Each house was painted a different shade, from the palette of pastel colours which had painted the larger and better-kept buildings of the downtown area. The colours gleamed gently in the bright light and Lee, without sunglasses and without her hat, was glad that someone at some time in the past had decreed that all buildings on the island should be painted in pale shades rather than white, to cut down the amount of glare.

By the time she reached the top of the street she was breathless and the black cloud was in front of her eyes again, but after a short rest she was able to walk along the other street of small houses. Although shabby they were neat and clean, showing, like the whole of Willemstad, the

Dutch concern for neatness and cleanliness.

At last she came to the house where she hoped to find Adrian and, with her heart thumping excitedly, she went up the wooden steps to the verandah. A doorway covered in fine mesh faced her, and through the mesh she could see into a dark passageway. Opening the mesh door, she knocked on the wooden inner door and waited.

A small boy appeared. He was ochre-coloured, had crinkly black hair and huge brown eyes. When he saw Lee his eyes nearly popped out of his head and he darted back down the passage into the recesses of the house before she could speak to him.

Next a girl of about sixteen appeared, dressed in a dress of brightly printed cotton, her dark hair drawn back into two tight pigtails tied at the ends with red ribbons. Her skin had a olive tint, and her eyes were also big and brown. There was no doubt as to her relationship to the small boy.

'What do you want?' she asked in Dutch.

'I am looking for Adrian Hartog,' said Lee slowly in the same language. She had been rehearsing the speech all the way from the Van Breedan store.

The girl's eyes popped as the little boy's had done. Turning back into the house she shrieked one word—'Muder.' Coming back, she pushed open the screen door and invited Lee to enter the hallway.

There was a smell of something spicy being cooked and it made Lee realise how hungry she was. With the feeling of hunger came the black cloud again, and she leaned against the wall hoping her faintness was not apparent.

A door opened at the end of the passage and a small woman came forward. She walked quickly and spoke sharply in that strange language, the mixture of several other languages Lee had heard Max Van Breedan using. The girl answered in the same language and waved her hand

26

in Lee's direction.

The woman advanced. Head tilted back, she stared up at Lee. Her face was prematurely wrinkled, her dark hair grizzled with grey, but her dark brown eyes glinted with fury.

'You know where that no-good Hartog is?' she snapped in broken English.

'No. The girl misunderstood,' said Lee, feeling a little taken aback by the reference to Adrian as "no-good". 'I'm looking for him. I was told he lived here.'

'I am looking for him too.' The woman turned her head aside and made a good imitation of spitting as if to express her opinion of Adrian. 'He leave here tree—no, four weeks ago, and not come back. He not pay his rent for two months before that. When he go he take all our savings with him.'

'Oh, no!' Lee could not bite back the exclamation of horror at this insinuation that Adrian was a thief.

'Oh, yes,' jeered the woman, imitating the English accent. 'He take my niece—Josita—too, my sister's daughter who I look after since she was a baby. Who are you? His sister?'

'No, no, just a friend of his,' replied Lee, shrinking back against the wall, afraid of that fury as she coped with the unpleasant truth. Adrian wasn't here. Adrian was a thief as well as a liar. 'Have you any idea where he is now?' she asked.

'Idea?' The woman looked puzzled for a moment, obviously not understanding the idiomatic phrase.

'Do you know where he has gone?' asked Lee slowly. Her head was whirling again and she was afraid she might fall down.

'He tell me one time he get a job in Maracaibo maybe, and he go there,' said the woman.

'Where is that?'

'Venezuela. Across the water,' was the reply.

27

At that moment there was the sound of heavy footsteps on the verandah. The screen door opened and a big man wearing a construction worker's round hard hat entered. He was not as dark-skinned as the woman and his facial features showed his Dutch origins. He glanced in surprise at Lee, shot a question at the woman who told him quickly why Lee was there.

He turned and looked at Lee again. There was an expression of sadness in his eyes.

'Your friend has gone, miss,' he said quietly. 'He was not a good friend to us. He stole our money and Josita.'

'I'm sorry,' said Lee faintly. She tried to blink the black cloud away again, but it wouldn't go. This time it came down and enveloped her, and she could no longer see.

CHAPTER TWO

SHE was lying on something soft and there were voices speaking. It sounded like that record being played backwards again. Lee opened her eyes and found she was lying on a sofa in a small room which seemed to be crammed with furniture, most of it made from bamboo. The voices were coming from the two people who were hovering near her, the woman and man who had told her that Adrian had not been a good friend to them, because he had stolen their savings and their niece.

The man went out of the room and the woman came across to her. The dark brown eyes which had glinted with fury now had an anxious expression.

'You okay?' the woman asked cautiously. It seemed to Lee that she looked a little frightened.

'Yes,' she whispered, and lifted her head. It felt heavy and ached abominably, so she laid it back again on the cushion. 'What happened?'

'You faint,' said the woman, 'but everything all right. We send for your friend.'

Puzzled, Lee closed her eyes. Her friend? Who could that be? She had no friend in Curaçao. Once she had thought she had; once she had thought to find Adrian. But he had gone away with another woman, with the niece of this woman who was hovering over her so anxiously. He had betrayed her trust. Tears of weakness welled up behind Lee's eyelids and she groaned. At once the woman began to chatter agitatedly, like a small parrot, asking the same question over and over again. 'You okay? You okay?'

'Yes, I'll be all right in a few minutes,' Lee murmured

reassuringly. 'Could I have a drink of water, please?'

'*Ja, ja*. I go at once to fetch it.' The woman scurried out, and alone at last Lee opened her eyes and let the tears run down her cheeks.

The room was very hot and stuffy. Somehow she must get out of it and away from the house before 'her friend' came; she couldn't for the life of her think who the friend might be. Slowly she raised her head again. The pain in it was not quite as bad as it had been. Struggling to a sitting position, she swung her feet to the floor, and sat waiting to see if the walls swayed or the floor tilted or if the black cloud came back. Nothing happened, but the urge to move had died and she sat there slumped, waiting for the water to come, wishing it were a dream she was having and that soon she would find herself back in the hotel, waking up that morning and looking forward to finding Adrian.

How long she sat waiting for the woman to return with the water she did not know, but the door opened at last and she looked up expecting to see the small dark woman. Instead Max Van Breedan walked in. He was wearing an elegantly-cut jacket which matched his light grey trousers and the knot of his tie was in the correct place against his crisp black shirt. In one hand he held a gilt-rimmed pair of dark glasses; he looked suave and sophisticated and businesslike.

Behind him came the small woman, carrying a glass of water. In the open doorway the small boy and the girl hovered, their eyes round as they stared at Max.

Surprise held Lee still and silent. The small woman chattered to Max in the strange mixed-up language, her attitude one of deference. He stood with his head tipped forward, his eyes veiled as he listened, and when the woman had finished talking he took the glass from her, said something in the same language and smiled at her. The woman smiled back, glanced quickly at Lee, murmured, '*Ja,*

30

meneer,' and turning, scuttled to the door, shooing the boy and the girl away with gestures of her hands and fierce exclamations.

The door closed. Max Van Breedan moved towards Lee and held out the glass to her. She took it from him, sipped some water and then said,

'Why are you here?'

'When you fainted they were very worried,' he answered evenly. 'They found a piece of paper in your hand with their address on it; it also had the name of the company on it. Josita, their niece, used to work in the store, so they knew how to get in touch with the personnel department. The woman they phoned recognised the description of you, told me what had happened, and I drove over straight away.' He paused, then added slowly, 'I guess they told you that Hartog had left taking their money and Josita with him.'

'Yes,' she whispered. She couldn't look up and again tears of weakness were springing in her eyes. 'Oh, I've been so silly!' she wailed suddenly, dropping the glass and putting her hands to her face.

Sobs shook her violently. She was vaguely aware of him moving, then the sofa sank beneath his weight as he sat down beside her. Suddenly she found herself leaning against something warm and firm while a bar of iron held her. Relieved by a sense of security that the bar of iron gave her, she let the tears flow, finding ease in letting go.

Gradually her sobs subsided, and she gave a long sigh. No one spoke to her and no one seemed to want her to move, so she just lay there in an exhausted daze listening to the drumbeat which was just beneath her ear. After a while she realised that the drumbeat was actually a heart-beat, that the damp stuff under her cheek was a black shirt covering a vital body, and that the bar of iron which had been holding her was a tensile muscular arm.

31

Opening her eyes cautiously, she looked up straight at the angle of a square jaw and the curve of an enigmatic mouth. The mouth was enigmatic, Lee decided, because it didn't go with the solidity of the other features; it had a tendency to curve generously, almost passionately, and this tendency was kept under by a strict control which had created deep lines at its corners and thinned the sensual fullness of the lower lip.

'I'm sorry,' she apologised to that mouth, and saw it quirk slightly at the corner with sardonic humour.

'So you should be! You've frightened the life out of two very good hardworking people. You've also soaked my shirt.'

The light, black-fringed eyes glinted wickedly as he slanted a glance down at her.

'I've never fainted in my life before,' she averred, pushing away from him and sitting up.

'You've probably never gone without food for such a long time before, nor had such a shock,' he replied. 'If you'd like to blow your nose and comb your hair, I'll take you out of here and feed you. Your handbag is over there on the table—I presume you do have a handkerchief and a comb?'

'Yes.' Lee stood up and went over to the table. She felt weak—an odd floating sensation which made everything around her, including the man, seem slightly unreal. 'Mr Van Breedan,' she said, turning to face him, 'you don't have to feed me. I can manage very well by myself now. I won't faint again.'

Ignoring her, he stood up and glanced at the gold watch which gleamed on his dark wrist.

'If we leave now we should miss the worst of the usual midday traffic, so be quick. You'll be able to wash your face at the restaurant. But do comb your hair, there's a good girl.'

'Mr Van Breedan——' she began, furious because he

was treating her as if she were twelve instead of twenty-two.

'Miss Williams,' he interrupted her suavely, 'I hope you're not going to put on another brave show of independence, because I'm beginning to find it boring.'

'It isn't a show!' she spluttered.

'No?' The irony in his voice made her want to scratch and spit at him like an angry cat. 'Then let me put your mind at ease. I feel it is my duty to the community at large to prevent you from fainting again by feeding you. When you're full of good food you might feel more comfortable, and you might begin to behave with more common sense. Then I shall put my proposition to you.'

In the middle of combing her hair Lee stopped, and with her arm still raised she glanced at him suspiciously. The word proposition alarmed her.

'Proposition?' she repeated carefully.

He returned her gaze blandly, his face impassive.

'No need for you to look at me like that! I'm not a saint by any means, but I've nothing unpleasant in mind. It has just occurred to me that you and I could come to an arrangement which would help us both solve a problem.'

'A business arrangement?' she asked cautiously as she put her comb in her bag.

'But of course. I never make any other kind of arrangement,' he replied with a touch of self-mockery. 'Are you ready now?'

'Mr Van Breedan——' she began again, and he groaned.

'In a groove, Miss Williams?' he countered as, disconcerted by his groan, she hesitated. 'If you can say nothing else but "Mr Van Breedan", may I suggest you stop talking altogether and we'll go and eat.'

A big hand closed round her bare arm just above the elbow and she was forced to go with him across the room and into the hall. There the woman was waiting, and Max said a few words to her. They sounded kind and reassuring, but they were totally unintelligible to Lee. The woman answered again with deference, and Lee's last impression of the little house was of two heads bobbing in the gap left by the half-opened door at the end of the passage as the two children watched her departure.

The car was a surprise. It was the latest model of a certain exclusive European sports car, pale blue in colour, and its roof was down. On the seat beside the driver's was her white sun-hat.

'Put it on,' ordered Max Van Breedan, and she obeyed. But as soon as they swept forward down the hill, the wind of their swift passage lifted the hat from her head and she had to put up her hands to catch it. At once her hair swirled in a blaze of copper-coloured silk, wafting sideways in front of the driver's face and curling round his shoulders, and she had to pull it back. Jamming the hat down on her head, she held it on with both hands.

Dazzle danced in diamond-bright flashes along the chromium bumpers of cars. Traffic lights changed to red. The car stopped. Pedestrians crossed in front of it: laughing girls with dark shiny faces who were dressed in bright clothes; business men in lightweight suits; tourists in crisp white, red and blue.

'Everyone is going home for their midday meal, and some will take a siesta. Most of the stores close from noon until two,' explained Max, as the car shot forward when the lights changed to green.

'Do you have a siesta?' Lee asked, surprised to find that the latin habit was carried on in a Dutch country.

'That depends entirely on whom I have lunch with,' he replied coolly, and she felt a little as if she had been prying into his personal life. 'Look to your right,' he continued in the same impersonal way. 'Does the yellow-and-white building look familiar to you?'

She glanced at a handsome citron-coloured building and felt memory stir.

'It looks like one I've seen in Amsterdam.'

'Correct. It's the Mikve Israel Emmanuel Synagogue, and is a copy of the temple in Amsterdam. Portuguese Jews came here by way of Holland when they were being persecuted. That's the oldest Jewish shrine in the Western Hemisphere.'

'Curaçaons seem to be a mixture of many different races,' she said.

'More than fifty,' he agreed, 'even the British were here for a while.'

'Are there any of the original inhabitants left?'

'Arawaks, you mean? Not any pure-bred ones, unfortunately. They died out in the last century. But they gave the island its name, and you can see them surviving in the features of many of the islanders.'

While he was talking the car had been moving in a series of spurts through the midday rush of traffic. To Lee's surprise their way took them over the drawbridge and past the hotel where she had stayed the night. On they went in the direction of the harbour, and she could see a bridge lifting in a green arc spanning the water between two blocks of land. Soon they were sweeping into the courtyard of an old building that looked as if it had once been a military fort and was set on a hill overlooking the harbour and the town.

They were greeted in the entrance of the restaurant by the proprietor, who knew Max and was glad to see him, judging by his effusive flow of words. Lee was shown to the ladies' room and there among hygienic smells and shining tiles she dutifully washed her face and hands.

Like a good girl, she thought wryly to herself, who was being taken out to lunch by a beneficent citizen of Willemstad as his duty to the community at large. But she didn't want to be treated as a girl. She wanted to be treated as the woman she was, as an equal.

But to be the equal of Max Van Breedan she would have to be a business woman, the type of woman she had seen in London as well as Amsterdam; well-dressed, well-coiffured, well-manicured, wearing the latest in elegantly tailored clothes, as suave and sophisticated on the outside, and just as hard inside, as he was. A gentle musician like herself, given to foolish impulses and a mind full of romantic notions, was no match at all for Max Van Breedan.

No more than she had been a match for Adrian Hartog, liar and thief. Lee's mouth trembled uncontrollably and tears threatened as the thought of Adrian's behaviour brought with it a dragging feeling of disillusionment. Before it could overwhelm her again she went from the room back to the entrance hall.

From a glassed-in terrace there was a panoramic view of Sint Anna Baie, which joined the sea to the big inland harbour. Max pointed out the old pontoon bridge, Queen Emma as he called it, which at one time had held up all the traffic wanting to cross from the Punda to the Otrabunds whenever a sea-going ship had sailed up the baie and into the harbour. Now Emma was a showpiece because the new bridge leapt in a high arc over the main channel, so that the flow of traffic could continue while a ship passed underneath it.

Max ordered the meal. It was a local dish called *Kapucijners Garni*. Browned Dutch peas with onions mixed with tasty morsels of smoked bacon were served with a hamburger steak and accompanied by many side dishes of pickles. Lee could not eat it all. To do that she would have had to have starved for four days, not almost twenty-four hours, she thought humorously as she took a sip of the ice-cold locally brewed beer from a tall glass stein.

Her companion was having a second beer and had finished eating. He didn't seem to have much to say, and was now sitting back in his chair casually smoking a cigar while he watched the many people who were having their midday meal in the sun-yellow air-conditioned room with its touches of Delft tiling and the trailing greenery of indoor plants. The noise of conversation and the clatter of cutlery and dishes were cheerful everyday sounds which made Lee feel comforted, less worried. As she looked around, again her quick ears caught the sound of the strange garbled language.

'What is the language so many people here speak?' she asked, wanting to bring Max's attention back to herself.

He glanced at her.

'Papiementu. It's a *patois* developed from Portuguese, Dutch and Spanish with a few English, African and Indian words thrown in. Everyone speaks it and even newspapers are printed in it. It's the only primitive language to develop in modern times—even the great literature of the world is translated into it, and most of the folk songs of the island are sung in it. Nearly all the people of the islands are quadrilingual, speaking Dutch, English, Spanish and Papiementu with equal ease. But Dutch is the official language. Have you had enough to eat?'

'Yes, thank you. It was very good,' she said politely.

'What are you going to do now that you've discovered Hartog has eloped with the pretty Josita?' he asked casually.

'I'll have to look for a job, to earn some money to pay my fare back to England,' Lee replied, looking at him steadily.

'Well done,' he praised softly and ironically, 'that was said in the great British tradition of showing grit and determination when faced with great odds. Obviously you've no idea of what looking for a job in these islands is like.

37

Why do you think Hartog left? Because even he, a Dutch national, would have problems getting work without good references. There's already a large work force here and a shortage of employment. You're an alien, here on a visitor's permit, and I'm warning you you're going to draw a blank. No one will employ you.'

'I thought I might get a job as a performer,' she said. 'In a club or a restaurant.'

His glance was pitying as he surveyed her through cigar smoke.

'I hate to think of the sort of place which would take you on,' he said slowly. 'I think you'll find all the accredited hotels and clubs already have performers in your line. Remember that we're close to South America here and the people from Venezuela and Brazil were born with music in their blood, so there's no shortage of individuals or groups who can sing and play guitars.'

'Then I'll just have to take my chance with them, won't I?' she retorted lightly, although secretly she felt a little daunted by what he had said.

Max gave her a sardonic glance which she returned with a clear direct one of her own. He was used to having his own way, she could see that: he was probably used to having his advice taken immediately too, and he didn't like her refusing to take what he offered.

'Where did you stay last night?' he asked next. He was full of questions, she thought with a touch of exasperation, but it wasn't the first time she had come up against the Dutch concern for details and their sheer curiosity. She told him and he made a grimace. At once she was up in arms.

'Where else could I stay? It was cheap and clean. The people were kind. They didn't ask a lot of questions,' she retaliated.

'Implying that I'm not kind, and I ask too many ques-

38

tions,' he countered with a quirk of humour. 'The place you stayed in is not in an area where a girl with your attractive appearance and openness of manner can stay for long without some sort of unpleasant pass being made at you. Seamen from all over the world stay in that hotel, and some of them don't always stop to think before they act.'

'Do you know of anywhere else I could stay?' she asked more meekly, recalling the leers of the few men who had been standing about outside the hotel when she had left it that morning. 'It wouldn't have to be too expensive.'

He tapped the ash from his cigar into the ashtray, seemingly engrossed in watching the coil of grey ash disintegrate as it touched smooth glass. His eyelashes were fans of black against the swarthy sun-bronzed skin of his face, hiding whatever expression was in the light eyes, and giving him the appearance of a suave devil planning some dark and devious plot.

'You could stay with me ...'

'Stay with you?' Lee interrupted angrily. 'Only a few seconds ago you were warning me that an unpleasant pass might be made at me in the place where I was staying last night, and now you suggest I stay with you! Really, Mr Van Breedan, I ... er ... well, words fail me,' she finished lamely as he looked up at her suddenly, his eyes murder-bright.

'I'm glad they do,' he retorted icily, 'because that means I can finish what I was going to say without fear of any more interruptions. You could stay with me as my wife.'

It was as if he had thrown a hand grenade at her. There was a blinding flash inside her head, and stars danced before her eyes.

'You look shattered, Miss Williams,' he scoffed.

'I am,' she gasped. 'You don't ... you can't ask someone you've just met to be your wife! Marriage isn't a business arrangement.'

'For me, it is. There is a contract to be signed, terms to be drawn up, accepted and upheld,' he retorted quietly. 'Being a businessman I'm an opportunist. I am also something of a fatalist, a trait handed down to me, I suspect, by my South American mother. Today you have turned up out of the blue, and in your let-down, half-starved, poverty-stricken state you present a solution to a problem which has been bothering me for some time. You arrived here expecting to be married, all prepared to take the important step, but the man you expected to marry has gone. I, on the other hand, have to marry before the end of this week. I suggest we amalgamate. In other words I'm asking you to marry me.'

His cool approach repelled and fascinated her at the same time. She glanced round quickly as if afraid someone might be listening or watching, but no one was paying any attention to them. Then she looked at the man on the other side of the table. He had picked up his beer stein and was draining it, looking as calm as if proposing marriage to young women who strayed into his office was something he did every day.

'Why do you have to get married before the end of this week?' she asked.

'I'm being blackmailed into it,' he answered curtly.

'Blackmailed?' she whispered. Her eyes were wide as she imagined all sorts of Mafia-like intrigues. 'Oh, who would do a thing like that to you?'

'A very stubborn old man. My father, Vincent Van Breedan,' he said. 'He had only two sons, and since my brother is now dead I'm the last of a line—of a business dynasty in fact—and I'm a bachelor. When Bruno was alive it didn't matter that I'd chosen to stay a bachelor because I like my freedom, but now I find I'm not only responsible for my brother's daughter—her guardian in fact—but also my single state and style of life is worrying my father.'

40

He stopped speaking and once again his eyes were hidden as he regarded the ash at the end of the cigar. The muscles in his jaw tightened visibly, pulling the skin taut across his cheeks, accentuating the strong angle of bone as he controlled some emotion.

'He is very ill,' he continued slowly, 'and not likely to live much longer. Before he dies he would like to be sure that there is a possibility of the dynasty being secured through my sons. He has asked me to get married. Do you think you could help me to make him happy for the last few weeks, or possibly months, of his life?'

Absolutely astounded by his request, Lee watched strong blunt-ended fingers squash the remains of the cigar into the ashtray. She was imagining an old man, racked with pain, trying to impose his will on this other strong-willed man, using wits which had been sharpened in a lifetime in trade and, in the end, having to appeal to what was probably the only soft spot in Max Van Breedan's character; his loyalty to and his affection for his father.

'There must be other women you could ask,' she said, guessing instinctively that no man as attractive and as wealthy as he was would be without women friends.

Again she felt the shock of that upward lightning-bright glance.

'There are,' he replied dryly, his mouth twisting a little cynically. 'There are even some who would sell their souls to be asked. But none of them are nice, young and innocent like you. And none of them are English.'

'What has my being English to do with it?' she demanded.

'My father's mother was English. Marry a nice English girl like your grandmother, was his last instruction issued to me the last time I saw him. You arrive today, nice, young, innocent and English—both my opportunism and

41

my fatalism tell me you must be the one. It's as simple as that.'

He was very clever, Lee thought. She liked being told she was nice and innocent, was pleased to know that such qualities in the female sex were still admired, even if it was only by an old man. Then there was the way he had worded his request; it appealed to her generosity, her concern for the happiness of other people. Could she help him make it possible for his father to die happy? If she refused could she live with herself afterwards? For it would be on her conscience for the rest of her life.

But marriage, and all it implied, to this cold calculating business machine; marriage without love to a man she had just met and wasn't sure she even liked; surely it was impossible for someone like herself?

'Isn't it like practising deception to marry someone you've just met so as to make your father happy?' she demurred. Max nodded.

'Possibly. But sometimes deception is necessary to make someone happy, to give them ease. I'm sure there must have been times in your life when you've told a white lie to avoid distressing someone you've loved and respected.'

From which of his forebears had he inherited his devilish perspicacity, she wondered, the Dutch, the English or the South American?

'You're making it awfully difficult for me to refuse,' she scolded him, and his mouth twitched with humour.

'But of course. That is my intention,' he replied. 'Look at it in another way. In return for marrying me you'll be able to live in a comfortable house, receive an allowance and have a pleasant time on a tropical island. Curaçao isn't a paradise, but it has attractions. Then there are the other islands—Aruba with its beautiful beaches, Bonaire with its wild birds. Have you ever seen pink flamingoes in flight? Marry me and I promise you you shall.'

'I'm not a child who has to be tempted by promised sweets,' she rebuked him gravely.

'What are you, then?' His eyebrows, which had strange peaks on them, lifted derisively as he scanned her face before letting his glance drift lower to her bare slim throat, thence to the shapes of her slight breasts outlined by the pinafore bodice of her dress. 'If you're a woman, prove it by behaving in a mature way,' he added. 'Put self and prejudice aside to help me make an old man happy.'

'I'm not prejudiced,' she objected hotly. She had always prided herself on her lack of prejudice.

'Of course you are. You're prejudiced against me because I had the foresight to sack your beloved Adrian before he could start embezzling company money. You're prejudiced because you believe he would still be here if I hadn't sacked him. You're also prejudiced against me because I'm a dark southerner and my colouring rouses all your northern antipathy. And you're prejudiced right now because I wish to marry you for convenience, not for love. I wouldn't mind betting that you've made up your mind to dislike me even before you know me very well.'

'Well, can you honestly say you like me?' she countered, more shaken than she cared to admit by his astute listing of her feelings about him.

'How could I dislike you?' he drawled softly, his glance drifting over her in a way which disturbed her more than anything he had said, so that she had to subdue a strong desire to get up and rush from the restaurant. 'Physically you're extremely attractive. You're also the answer to a prayer I've been sending up for the best part of a week. Come now, what do you say? Shall we be married the day after tomorrow?'

'So soon?' The question came out in a shocked whisper.

'My father is dying, and so every hour, every minute counts. I can arrange the ceremony to take place on Friday

43

in the Civil Registration Building. It will be nothing complicated and quite private.'

She glanced away from him, out of the window. The red roofs of the old buildings in the city shimmered under the midday sun. Beyond the limit of the city sparse vegetation covered the coral which overlaid the volcanic rock from which the island was formed, and weird-looking trees bent at right angles to the steady north-eastern trade wind which pointed their heads inevitably towards the southwest. It was an arid, inhospitable-looking place, yet thousands of people lived there, clinging to it with a tenacity which was characteristic of their Dutch forebears.

Could she—no, rather, should she—marry this man she had just met? Was it right to marry without love? All Lee's dearly-held views on the subject of marriage suggested that it wasn't right. She loved Adrian and should be marrying him this week, not a stranger.

She looked at Max Van Breedan. He was watching her, his eyes as grey as glass, his face as solid and uncommunicative as that of a bronze statue. He had been right. His southern darkness did rouse a primitive reaction in her, a fear of something foreign.

But if she didn't accept his proposal what alternative was there for her now that Adrian had gone? She could walk the streets of Willemstad, looking for work without much hope of finding it. Her spirit quailed a little at the prospect. How often would she be turned away with a polite refusal? How long would her small amount of money last? How soon would it be before the authorities closed in on her and asked her to leave the island, or deported her?

'Couldn't you give me a job in your company? I could work as a sales assistant. I have some experience, I used to serve in a shop in London during my vacations,' she said, glancing at him hopefully.

'No, I couldn't. There are no suitable vacancies,' he

44

replied with a blunt finality which made her realise it was useless for her to pursue that line further. 'Why don't you regard my proposal as a job? Marriage is as much a career for a woman as any other work is. It has to be worked at for it to be successful. The allowance I would give you would be your wages.'

Marriage as a career? The whole idea was distasteful to her romantic outlook. Marriage wasn't even an alternative to a career in her opinion. It was a wonderful, mysterious uniting of two people who wished to live together because they loved each other.

'Put any romantic notions out of your head for a few moments,' he urged quietly, and she glanced at him in alarm. He seemed to know what she was thinking. 'Look at it as I do, in a businesslike way. I need a wife—*pronto*—at once. You need a job. Now go on from there and give me an answer yes or no.'

He had brought the whole situation down to basic terms. The least she could do was follow his lead.

'I have to think about it,' she said slowly. 'And I'd have to make sure for myself that there is no alternative before I can give you an answer.'

He thought about that, eyes hidden again as he glanced at the bill which the waiter had just presented to him. He took out a leather wallet, extracted a credit card and handed it with the bill to the waiter, who went away.

Elbows on the table, Max leaned forward to pin her down with his sharp glance.

'It's a pity you didn't stop to think before deciding to fly out here,' he taunted softly. 'But no doubt you'll tell me that love doesn't stop to think. All right, I'll give you until four o'clock tomorrow afternoon to think. Do you want to start searching for alternatives now, or shall I take you back to your hotel?'

The waiter came back with the credit card and a slip of

paper to be signed. When it was signed Max rose to his feet and Lee stood up too. She longed to go back to the hotel to rest for a while, but it was probably in her best interests to start looking for a job immediately.

'I'd like to go back to town,' she said. 'Thank you very much for the meal. Where shall I find you tomorrow afternoon to give you an answer?'

'You know where my office is,' he replied curtly.

He dropped her off in one of the main shopping streets and she spent a tiring and fruitless afternoon job-hunting. Eventually she gave up and, after having a small meal in a cheap café, she walked back to the hotel beside the canal-like inlet from which the floating market had sailed away.

That night, in the little room at the hotel, lying on the creaking bed, was one of the worst Lee had ever known in the whole of her life. The walls of the room were thin and she could hear the person in the next room turning in bed and occasionally snoring. Without air-conditioning the room seemed unbearably warm, making it difficult for her to doze off. Unused to such heat, she lay perspiring, tormented by disturbing thoughts.

Nothing had gone as she had hoped. Adrian had betrayed her trust in him, and now she was alone in a strange country with very little money and not much prospect of earning any. It was enough to make the most optimistic person depressed and apprehensive.

She sat up and turned the pillow over, hoping to find the other side cooler for her head. Lying down again, she closed her eyes tightly, determined to sleep. A new thought came. In a way she had been fortunate; she had been offered a job. As a wife! Her mouth twisted ruefully, as the thought extended itself. As a wife to a formidable man of business; a man who did not suffer fools gladly, who had had no hesitation in sacking Adrian; a man who seemed to be made of ice, he was so lacking in emotion.

46

Desperately she turned again on the hard bed, trying to close Max Van Breedan out of her thoughts, but it was impossible. She kept asking questions about him and finding no answers, which left her with a longing to see him again, to be with him for a while and to find out the answers to those questions.

Had he ever been in love? Had he ever been riotously happy or miserably sad? Was the business machine of his brain always in control? Did he ever give way to impulse?

His dark impassive face, his cold light eyes, gave the impression that he was totally without feelings of any sort, and in her imagination Lee saw his life up to that point in time as a flat plain on which the only high landmarks were his successes in business. Then she remembered that enigmatic mouth of his which hinted at passion kept under firm control; she remembered the way his face had changed, and had lit up with attractive devilry when he had laughed into the phone in his office. Beneath the veneer of solidity and reliability, beneath the thick layer of ice, there lurked a latin devil who, if he were aggravated too much, might burst forth one day with all the attendant fire and brimstone and devastate anyone who had provoked him.

Under the thin sticky sheet Lee shivered a little, in spite of the heat, at the image she had created. There would be danger in giving in to the temptations offered by such a person, and instinct warned her that if she agreed to marry him she would never be able to call her soul her own again.

Morning was bright with sunlight as once more she walked across the bridge. By midday she was finding the sidewalks hard, the sun too hot, and the air too dry. Her feet ached, her head ached and her body was craving liquid refreshment. She had had no luck—she had been to every place which offffered entertainment and had discovered Max Van Breedan had been right. No one required a performer. Nor did they require a dishwasher, a chambermaid or a

47

waitress. They had local people lined up for jobs like that, and had no wish to employ an alien.

She had a soft drink at one of the outdoor cafés and decided to go to the big hotel which was built within the strong walls of the old fortress on the point, jutting out at the end of the bay into the sea. Once again she drew a blank. Leaving the hotel, she wandered through an archway in the thick old walls on to a narrow beach.

Shining breakers of white-laced sun-shot green water thundered on to the shingle and withdrew to build up into new crested billows before flinging themselves again at the obdurate land. Cut off from the town by the thick reddish-brown wall of the old fortress, alone except for an old man who was sitting propped against the wall, his flat-crowned straw hat tipped forward over his eyes as he enjoyed his siesta, Lee watched the tumbling water and went back in time imagining the place being stormed by pirates. Cannon from the old fort must have belched forth flame and smoke as the defenders of the town tried to sink the pirate ship.

But the ship she could see beyond the foaming combers' hove-to on the glittering expanse of blue sea, was no sailing ship with rakish masts and square sails. It was a cruise ship, so close to the land that it seemed to tower over it like a silver and white colossus, and the sight of it brought her back to the present and her problem.

She glanced at her watch. Siesta time was over. She had a little less than two hours to search for an alternative to the job Max Van Breedan had offered her. She went back to the town, and this time she had a little more luck because the girl in the cash desk at a restaurant took pity on her, and suggested she would never get a job until she went to the local employment authority.

Leave no stone unturned. Her grandmother's saying was coming in very useful lately, but after waiting almost an hour at the office of the authority for an interview, she was told coldly and politely that since she had entered the country without a permit she was regarded as a tourist, so she could stay no longer than fourteen days and must not look for or accept any work. A request for a working permit could only be taken into consideration if it was filed through a local employer who had offered her a job.

It looked as if she were caught in a vicious circle from which there was only one way of escape. So, with a sigh of resignation, Lee made her way to the entrance door of the building. It was almost four o'clock. She would have to go to Max Van Breedan, admit that she was defeated and accept his offer of work. It was the only way.

The glass of the entrance door flashed in the sunlight as it swung open and she went out. A tall figure loomed beside her. A deep voice said,

'Your time is up.'

Startled, she looked round. With dark glasses hiding his eyes and enhancing everything that was latin about him—the olive-tinted skin, the curling black hair, the wide ironic mouth, the haughtily flaring nostrils—he was the devil of her nocturnal imaginings and had appeared as suddenly, with Mephistophelean abruptness, but after all her wanderings she was very glad to see him.

'How did you know where to find me?' she asked. Perhaps he really had supernatural powers.

'Nothing to it,' he replied easily. 'I was passing by when I saw you come in here, so I waited for you to come out. Are you ready to give me an answer now?'

'Yes, I am,' she said with another sigh, thinking how wonderful it would be to have a bath or a swim in the ocean and then go to sleep. That would be heaven.

'We can't talk here,' he said. 'We'll go round the corner and have a beer at a sidewalk café. You can tell me all you've learned today.'

'I've learned that you were right,' she said as they

entered a wide street edged by pastel-coloured buildings, where only pedestrians were allowed and vehicular traffic was banned. 'I can't get a job without a work permit, and I can't stay without a residence permit. I can't leave because I've no money. I suppose you're always right?'

'Usually, not always,' he admitted coolly as he pulled out a chair for her at a table under a striped umbrella at a sidewalk café. 'Blisters?' he queried as she made a grimace.

'Yes. One of the straps on my sandal has been rubbing.'

'Because you have to find out the truth the hard way for yourself,' he scoffed as he sat down opposite to her.

A waiter, formally attired in black trousers, white shirt and bow tie and short red jacket, came to them. Beer was ordered, and not until he had brought and poured it did they speak again.

'Drink up,' ordered Max. 'Visitors to the islands often suffer from dehydration during the first few days. They don't realise that they must replace the liquid they lose through perspiration.'

The beer was ice cold and refreshing and his presence brought Lee a sense of comfort. She eased the troublesome sandal off her foot and let the pleasure of sitting there in the shade seep into her.

'Mr Van Breedan,' she began diffidently, because he did not seem disposed to speak first, 'would you tell me please what you would expect me to do if I marry you?'

He was in the process of lighting a cigar and she had to wait for his reply. When it was lit he blew out a cloud of smoke and surveyed her through it.

'So you're interested,' he murmured. 'I realise that because of the circumstances it wouldn't be a normal marriage, but I would like it to appear as normal as possible. So I would expect you to behave in public—that is, in front of my relatives and friends—as a newlywed woman normally behaves. I would also expect you to do what wives

50

usually do, show a preference for my company, go to social functions with me, entertain my friends and business associates. In Willemstad there won't be much in the way of actual housework for you to do because there is a house-keeper, but when we stay at the beach house on my father's country estate I'd expect you to keep house and cook meals. Can you cook?'

'Yes, quite well. Mr Van Breedan . . .'

'Are you in that groove again?' he interrupted her. 'I reckon we've known each other for approximately three and a half hours. In that time I've held you in my arms while you wept, bought you a meal and asked you to marry me, so I think it's time we dropped the formal approach. You can call me Max and I'll call you Lee. It's an odd name. Is it short for something?'

'Promise you won't laugh if I tell you?' she said warily.

'As bad as that, is it?' he replied with a mocking lift of his eyebrows. 'All right, I won't laugh.'

'It's short for Leonora,' she confessed.

'That's a Spanish name—I always thought English girls had names like Anne, or Jane or Elizabeth. How did you get it?'

'I told you my father was a musician and played the trumpet,' she said, and he nodded. 'Well, one of his favourite pieces of music was the third overture Beethoven wrote for the opera *Fidelio*, because there was a trumpet solo in it that he always played.'

'I remember. Leonora was the faithful wife in the opera who managed to get into the prison where her husband was, and saved his life.' Max looked thoughtful.

'That's right.'

'Then possibly you're well-named. You certainly showed a superabundance of faith in Hartog, when you flew out here to join him when he hadn't even written to you asking you to come,' he remarked sardonically, and she flinched.

'Are you satisfied with my outline of what the job will consist of?'

'There's just one more thing.' Heavens, how was she going to say it? It had been easy to discuss such a matter with young women of her own age, but how could she approach the matter of the physical side of marriage with this tough business man who was several years older than herself?

'You're wondering about what happens between us when we're not on show to the public,' he suggested coolly, and she looked up to meet his narrowed knowledgeable eyes.

'Yes. How did you guess?'

'You went pink,' he replied dryly. 'Go on, ask me what it is you want to know. We have to have conditions laid down clearly in a situation like this, then we both know where we stand.'

Making an effort to swallow her embarrassment, Lee spoke in a low voice, not looking at him.

'You told me that your father wants you to marry so that the family name will be continued through your sons. Does that mean . . . will you want me to . . . I don't think I could,' she finished in a rush, her cheeks glowing pinker.

'I've given some thought to the problem,' he replied slowly. 'I don't expect my father to live to see any of my sons, and this marriage is just to convince him that there is a *possibility* of my having sons, to show him I'm willing to settle down and have a family. But there's no particular rush in that direction. If you like you could make it a condition that we won't expect anything in that respect from each other, unless the time comes when we feel we would both like to have a child. That time might never come while my father is alive, and so if we decide to part after his death it will be easier for us if the marriage hasn't been consummated. Does a condition like that make it easier for you to come to a decision?'

She should have guessed he would be businesslike about it and she was grateful for his cool, calm attitude.

'Yes, thank you. Could you tell me something about your niece now? How old is she?'

'Sixteen,' he answered. 'She was badly hurt in the crash which killed my brother and she hasn't yet recovered properly from the shock. Her face was rather badly scarred by flying glass, which has had the effect of making her shrink from meeting people. I hope that having someone young like yourself to live with will help her.'

'Doesn't she have a mother?' Lee inquired.

'She has, somewhere.' His mouth twisted cynically and she gathered he did not have a very high opinion of Juliana's mother. 'Can I have your answer now? Yes or no?'

Pushed into a position where she had to make a considered decision instead of letting impulse push her into action, Lee did not shirk the responsibility. Keeping her mind steadily on the reason for this marriage, she raised her head and looked straight at him with clear eyes.

'Yes,' she said, and as soon as the word was out of her mouth she felt as if a great load had slipped off her shoulders. The die was cast. She was committed.

'Thank you,' he said in a matter-of-fact way. 'Now to details. My father, though ill, is still very shrewd. He will want to know where we met and which part of England you come from; he won't be pleased if he finds out we met for the first time yesterday. I was in England and in Amsterdam last year, so we could have met in either place. I had to return in a hurry because Bruno was killed, which could be the reason why we didn't marry over there. You promised to come out here when you could: it's just a matter of you substituting me for Adrian. Does it sound feasible to you?'

'Er . . . yes.' She must have sounded dubious because he

asked quickly:

'Is there anyone in England, a close relative of yours I should know about?'

'No. My father was an only son, and his mother died last year. I've lost touch with my mother's family.'

'In one way it's good, but in another it's bad,' he said thoughtfully. 'Vincent would probably prefer it if you could have presented him with a family tree showing all your forebears. Which part of the country did your father come from?'

'He was born in Wales. My mother came from Lincolnshire.'

'Aha!' Interest glinted in his eyes. 'I know of that. It's the fen country. Isn't a part of it called Holland, because it's very flat and the sea has to be kept out, as in the Netherlands?'

'Yes, that's right. And I believe Dutch people settled there in the past. At one time there were windmills there,' Lee smiled.

'Good. That will go down well with Vincent. He'll have you descended from Dutch emigrants to England in no time and that will make him happy. He'll believe you're like himself,' he said with a touch of dry humour. 'Now, if you've finished your beer I'll take you to collect your luggage from the hotel and to pay your bill. You can stay the night in the Van Breedan town house where I live. We'll be married tomorrow at ten o'clock, and afterwards I'll take you to meet my father, his sister Bertha, and Juliana. We'll stay a few days there see how it goes, and maybe fly to Aruba later. They'll expect us to have a honeymoon, you know.'

He was rushing her now that he had her word, and Lee would not have been normal if she had not tried to stall.

'How can we get married tomorrow? Don't you have to have a licence or something?' she gasped.

54

'I have one. I've been preparing for this for three weeks,' he replied with that ironic twist to his mouth. 'The only item missing has been an eligible woman. I seem to have found her. I suppose you have a suitable dress to wear?'

'Yes, I brought one with me,' she admitted.

'I thought you might have done. So there's nothing else to do except collect your stuff from the hotel, feed you, wash you and put you to bed for a good night's rest,' he said crisply.

'Oh! You make me seem like a child or a pet,' she objected, her eyes sparkling with anger. 'Perhaps I should make it clear to you that I'm a woman with a mind of my own, and if you think that just because I've agreed to marry you you've acquired a dumb passive slave who will automatically obey all your orders without questioning, then you're quite mistaken.'

For a few moments eyes the colour of golden sherry clashed with eyes the colour of ice-water. Then Max stood up in a leisurely way, and as he ground out his cigar in the metal ashtray, a mocking grin curved his mouth.

'Now I know why Adrian Hartog fled from Amsterdam,' he drawled. 'A woman with a mind of her own would be more than he could cope with. I suspect you're above his weight in a battle of wills between the two of you. But be warned, young one, you're not above mine. Shall we go now?'

His mocking comment made her seethe inwardly, but she stood up and followed him, walking back to the street where the blue car was parked. Within an hour her luggage and her precious guitar had been collected from the hotel where she had stayed for two nights, and the blue car was stopping outside an elegant eighteenth-century house on a quiet street on the Punda. The house was painted the same gingerbread colour as the company store and its gables were trimmed in white. Its gleaming white door swung open on oiled hinges and Lee entered a cool hallway from which a circular stairway with white wrought-iron balustrade curved to the upper floor.

Max introduced her to the severe-looking grey-haired woman who was the housekeeper, and then showed her upstairs to a room where a king-sized bed seemed to welcome her with open arms. A quick glance about the room assured her that it was utterly feminine, with frilled net curtains at the wide windows, a dainty dressing table with triple mirrors and pink rosebuds trailing over the wallpaper.

'Make yourself at home,' said Max in his cool way. 'I have to go back to the office to clear up several items of business as I shall be taking some time off.' Here his mouth dipped sardonically at one corner as he added, 'For a honeymoon, of course. I'll see you later. Meanwhile I suggest you have a belated siesta. You look as if you need it.'

The door closed quietly behind him as he left. Alone, Lee let her handbag slip to the floor and kicked off her sandals. Her bare toes curling on the soft deep pile of the rose-coloured carpet, she went over to the bed, drawn to it inexorably. She turned back the white rose-scented silken cover. Then, slipping off her dress and her underclothing, she slid beneath the cool crisp sheets.

It was like lying on a fluffy white cloud as it floated through the heavens, she thought drowsily. It was the most beautiful bed she had ever been in and nothing, not even the spirit-dragging, heart-pulling disillusionment which she was suffering as a result of Adrian's betrayal of her faith in him, could keep her awake any longer.

CHAPTER THREE

THE dress which Lee had chosen for her wedding to
Adrian Hartog was white, because she had always had a
secret wish to be married formally. It was a wish she had
kept secret because many of her friends at college had
tended to jeer at her love for tradition and ritual, calling her
old-fashioned. But it was not a long dress. Its full skirt fell
to her calves and was caught at the waist by a wide belt.
The top had a deep collar and revers edging the V-shaped
neckline and with full, sheer sleeves caught in at the wrists
with wide cuffs which echoed the belt. She had a white
wide-brimmed picture hat to go with it and white sling-
backed sandals with high heels to complete the outfit.

As she dressed alone in the big luxurious bedroom, she
felt a surge of regret that her wedding day was beginning
in such a cold, sterile way. There were no loving friends
and relatives fussing around, helping her to arrange her
hair, or telling her hat was at the wrong angle, or giving
her something new and blue to carry.

When she went downstairs into the hallway there was no
one there either, although Max had said he would meet her
there at nine-forty-five sharp. The previous evening she
had told him that it would be unlucky for him to take her
to the town hall and that they should go there separately,
but he had made no comment, merely given her one of his
penetrating stares and had wished her goodnight.

The front door opened suddenly. Cora de Palm entered.
She was dressed smartly in a suit of pink silk and had a
small pink hat clinging to her head. She stood staring for
a moment at Lee, then smiled in her kind way.

'I did not recognise you at first,' she said, 'you look so different in that dress. Are you ready to go now?'

Lee's eyes widened.

'With you?' she asked.

'But yes! The boss asked me to be a witness today and asked me to drive you to the town hall, because you are superstitious and do not wish to be driven there by him. I agree because, like you, I think it unlucky if you go together. Come now! My car is a saloon, so your hat will not be blown away as it would be in his.'

The arrival of Cora, the knowledge that Max had taken into consideration her own wishes and had done something to please her, made Lee's spirits lift a little. The drive through the bright sparkling streets of the clean city helped to raise them even further.

The place where the ceremony took place was another eighteenth-century building which had been restored to elegance. Max, wearing a light cream suit and cream shirt which enhanced his darkness, was waiting for her with the other witness, who was Franz Kuiperi, the chief accountant of the company. The ceremony was brisk and businesslike; a few words uttered quietly, a few names scratched on a document, and, surprisingly, a kiss from Max which she tried to dodge by dipping her head, so that it landed somewhere high on her right temple.

Her hand was shaken warmly by Cora, then briskly by Franz, and then they both went ahead, out of the room, so that when Lee and Max reached the hushed sunlit entrance hall it was empty and for a few minutes they were alone. Turning to her, he grasped her hand, pulled her towards him, and before she could dodge this time he kissed her slowly on the mouth, leaving her in no doubt that he was just as experienced in kissing as he was in buying and selling.

'A little practice does no harm,' he said as he released

her, 'that performance of yours in front of the registrar and the others nearly gave us away. Anyone who was interested would have guessed you had never been kissed by me. Now, next time we have to do it in front of spectators, don't duck.'

Her cheeks flaming, as a result not only of the demonstration of how to kiss but also in reaction to the reprimand, she went where he led her along a passage to a side door. Outside the blue car was parked on a quiet street and no one saw them leave. Since Lee's luggage and guitar had already been placed in the back of the car, they were able to set off straight away for the *Landhuis* belonging to Vincent Van Breedan, and soon they were darting in and out of the traffic making their way to the high bridge which soared in an arc a hundred and eighty feet above the entrance to the harbour.

Looking down through the protective railings which flickered past as the car sped over the bridge, Lee had a glimpse of a big oil freighter, its white deckhouses and red funnel bright against the deep blue of the water, looking like a child's toy from that great height as it moved slowly into the Schottegat, the superb, almost landlocked harbour.

The road curved down from the bridge, and something glittered over to the right beyond the water. Rows and rows of burnished oil storage tanks shimmered with dazzle as they reflected the sunlight and above them a pall of pale smoke drifted ever westwards from tall chimneys.

Lee curled the thumb of her left hand inwards to touch the band of gold which Max Van Breedan had placed on her third finger only half an hour previously. How long would it take for her to get used to wearing it? How long would it take for her to get used to being Mrs Van Breedan instead of Mrs Adrian Hartog?

Aaah! The cry was inside, deep down, silent, but straight from Lee's heart, produced by the pain she felt

59

because her wedding was nothing like she had imagined it would be. There was no warmth, no gaiety, no music, no flowers, but above all there was no Adrian. Instead there was this dark enigmatic stranger by her side, and he was whisking her away to goodness knows where. He had the right to do with her as he wished, and already she felt like one of his possessions instead of feeling like his partner.

Panic was an unpleasant taste in her mouth, both metallic and sour. She clasped her hands tightly together where they rested on top of the beautiful hat lying on her knees. Staring straight ahead, she fought a desire to open the door of the car and throw herself out, to escape from him before it was too late. Then she felt the wedding ring again. It *was* too late.

They had left the town behind. Before them the land stretched flat, arid, sparsely covered with green, ribbed with pale sand-coloured rock. Strange shapes reared up; blinking, Lee looked again, panic forgotten suddenly in amazement. Giant cacti, some like clusters of giant spiked fingers, others like large pincushions and others like huge jointed limbs, cast weird shadows on the dusty earth.

'They can't be real!' she exclaimed.

'What can't?' asked Max laconically.

'Those cacti.'

'They're real, all right. What else can you expect to grow in a place like this which has such a low rainfall, and where drinking water has to be distilled from sea water?'

'How can that be done?' The give and take of conversation was an anodyne for pain. She must keep it up and let the deep even flow of his voice soothe her fears.

'Desalinisation. There's a plant at Mundo Noba, the other side of Willemstad. It's the largest in the world and can produce four and half million gallons of water a day by evaporation, but the water which is produced is so pure it has to be run through limestone to give it a proper "water" taste. The cacti have other uses beside storing water—the datu, the big one, is used by the *kunekeros*, as we call the country people, to make fences round their property. You can see some over there.'

They were passing through a tiny village of houses clustered round a red-roofed church with a square tower. A few dusty palm trees provided shade, but mostly the land baked under the pitiless glare of the sun. Lee saw the fences Max mentioned, spiny limbs of cacti heaped together to make a protection. On the spines washing was hanging, and at one house she saw some animals, horned and bearded, tugging at the washing and eating it, and in some cases eating the fence.

'Oh, the goats are eating everything!' she gasped.

'How right you are,' he answered dryly. 'Although they are the main source of meat in the island they are also pests, and they eat everything in sight.'

Slowly the landscape was changing. Gentle hills billowed, as waves grow on the flat surface of the sea when it is touched by a strengthening wind. Thick tropical greenery tangled round the cacti in the shallow valleys, and soon feathery tamarind trees formed shady arches over the winding roadway. Small shrubs bearing what looked like small green apples grew everywhere. Max told her it was called machineel and that the fruits were poisonous.

Up and down the road dipped, and here and there on the hillsides Lee saw several old plantation houses all facing the sea. A hill bigger than any other appeared, a cone of gold; Lee asked for its name and learned that it was Sint Christoffel Berg, the highest peak in the islands at just over a thousand feet. Then they were turning their backs on it as Max guided the car off the road down a winding driveway edged by the feathery plumes of tamarind trees.

The drive ended in the courtyard of an old house built in traditional Dutch colonial style, with curved decorated

61

gables and an outside gallery which went all the way round it, on to which the long french windows of each room opened. In the centre of the red-tiled roof there was a circular tower with a clock in it, and a red-domed roof with a wind-vane.

They went in through the kitchen, which had red walls with white dots scattered all over them.

'Those are the eyes painted there by the slaves to scare the ghosts away,' explained Max, and turned to a small dark woman who was preparing some vegetables at the kitchen table. He spoke to her in Papiementu, gesturing to Lee—obviously explaining who she was—and the woman nodded, smiled and gabbled something unintelligible.

'This is Emma, and she says *bonbini*. That means welcome,' he said, and led Lee out of the kitchen down a passage into a big room like a central hall, the windows of which faced west. It was furnished comfortably but heavily, with big brocade-covered chesterfields and tables made from dark wood. Glass-fronted cupboards were ranged along the walls and family silverware and pewter as well as china glinted on their shelves.

An elderly woman was sitting in an armchair, doing some sort of needlework. She had a head of curly white hair and a tanned complexion, and was wearing a dress of brown linen edged with white at the neckline and sleeves. Gold-rimmed spectacles were perched on her nose, and she looked over them to see who had entered the room.

'Max!' she exclaimed, throwing down the embroidery and rising to her feet. 'I'm so pleased to see you. Many happy returns of the day.' She came to him and reached up to kiss him on the cheek he presented to her. Then she looked at Lee with inquisitive grey eyes. 'And who is this?' she asked.

It was hard not to stiffen when Max's arm slid possessively about her shoulders. The feel of his hand was hard and heavy, and Lee had a rebellious desire to shake it off. But he had said it was important that their relationship should appear to be normal before the members of his family, so she stood still and apparently submissive and smiled shyly at the older woman.

'This is Lee, Aunt Bertha,' he said. 'She and I were married this morning. I met her in England when I was over there last year.'

So might he have spoken about an item of merchandise he had bought on one of his buying trips, for all the emotion he showed, thought Lee a little wildly.

But if his announcement was a surprise to his aunt she did not show it either. Her comely face retained its serenity as she reached out a hand to Lee.

'Welcome,' she said in English. 'I wish you happiness. You too, Max.' Then with a sudden glint of mischievous humour in her eyes she added, 'You have been cradle-snatching, *meneer*.'

'Not really,' he replied smoothly. 'Lee is old enough to know her own mind and make her own decisions. How is Vincent today?'

'A little testy because it is your birthday and he had not heard from you. But your news will make him feel better. I suggest you go to see him to prepare him to meet Lee.'

Max nodded his agreement, murmured, 'I won't be long,' and went from the room.

'Come and sit over here, by this window. We have such a lovely view of the sea,' said Aunt Bertha. 'That island you can see in the distance is Aruba. You'll be staying for a few days, I expect?'

'I don't know. Max didn't say.' Lee felt suddenly foolish. Max should have told her how long they would be staying, or she should have asked him.

'No, I don't suppose he did,' said Aunt Bertha accommodatingly. 'And you don't know him well enough yet to insist on him telling you his plans. But I think he will want to stay a few days now he has come, so I'll go and tell Hannah to make up the beds in the beach house. I'm sure you'd like some coffee, too. The drive up from Willemstad is dusty.'

Having become used to the Dutch mid-morning *kopje koffie* when she had been living in Amsterdam, Lee accepted the offer gracefully and Aunt Bertha left the room.

Alone, she sat on the comfortable chair and looked round the room. The walls were painted pale blue, and a deeper blue carpet patterned in white and gold covered the floor. Pictures of sailing ships, dozens of them, cluttered the walls, and the tables and cabinets were crammed with lovely *objets d'art* collected by someone who knew their worth.

By one long window, which opened on to the long outside gallery, hung a guitar. Its golden wood gleamed against the pale blue wall, tempting her. Almost unknowingly, Lee rose to her feet and went across to touch it reverently, plucking one of its strings tentatively to find out if it was in tune.

'That belonged to my grandmother.'

The gruff girlish voice spoke in English, and she whirled to see a girl of about sixteen standing in the open window and gazing at her from under frowning eyebrows. The forward tilt of the head, the underbrowed stare were familiar, but otherwise there was no other resemblance to Max, for the hair was brown, streaked here and there by the strong sun, and the complexion of the plain, heavy-featured face was ruddy. In fact she looked as if she had been left out in the sun too long. She was wearing navy shorts and a blue cotton round-necked T-shirt, clothing which did nothing to flatter her over-plump figure.

'Hello,' said Lee in her usual open way. 'You must be Julian. Max told me about you. My name is Lee.'

'Are you his latest girl-friend? You don't look like the sort he usually brings with him.'

'No, I'm not. I . . . I'm his wife.' How strange it was to say!

Surprise lit the girl's eyes, which were a muddy greenish grey.

'You're joking,' she said.

'No, I'm not. Look.' Lee held out her left hand. The band of gold glinted in the sunlight.

Juliana stared at the ring, raised a hand and touched it with a curious finger. Then she looked back at Lee.

'That doesn't mean anything,' she retorted. 'He could have told you to wear that so he could say you're his wife. I know Uncle Max. He's very subtle.'

A little taken aback by this assessment of the man she had married, Lee hid a smile. She guessed Juliana had overheard an adult making the comment and had adopted it for herself.

'What makes you think I'd agree to go along with a trick like that?' she countered.

'He would make you. He can make anyone do anything he wants them to do,' replied the girl seriously, fingering the cruel scar which angled across her cheek as if trying to hide it.

'I expect you're right,' said Lee, 'but this time he wanted someone to be his wife and he chose me. We are really married. I have a certificate to show that we are, as well as a ring.'

The green eyes studied her sullenly for a moment, then Juliana smiled, an endearing smile that revealed that she had a gap between her two front top teeth.

'You're nice, and pretty,' she said. 'Can I call you Aunt Lee?'

'You can call me Lee if you like, because I don't feel old enough to be your aunt,' said Lee, laughing. 'This is a

65

beautiful guitar. Can you remember your grandmother? Did she used to play it?'

'I can't remember her. She died a long time ago. Even Uncle Max doesn't remember her. Aunt Bertha told me that Grandmother died when he was born—she wasn't very strong and shouldn't have had another baby.'

'Does anyone play the guitar now?' Lee asked.

'I haven't heard anyone play it. I'd like to play it, only there's never been anyone to show me how, and Grandfather won't let me touch it.'

'Didn't you ever ask your father if you could have one of your own?'

The heavy-featured face grew sullen again. The girl looked ready to run away at any minute, and Lee wished she had never mentioned her father.

'I asked him ... but he didn't listen,' Juliana muttered at last. 'And my mother is married to someone else now.'

'Doesn't she come to see you?'

'No. She doesn't like Grandfather. She ran away with another man.' This last was said almost defiantly.

'The one she married?'

'I think so. I'm not sure.'

'Ah, there you are, Julie.' Aunt Bertha had returned to the room carrying a tray on which there was a fine silver coffee service and some china cups and saucers. 'I was wondering where you were this morning. Have you introduced yourself to Lee, and do you know who she is?'

The girl nodded and began to back out of the room through the long open window. The flash of vivacity which had given her a fleeting prettiness had gone, leaving her looking dull and lumpish. Her heart touched by the apathy of the girl, Lee called out impulsively,

'I'll see you later, Julie, and we can talk some more about playing the guitar. I can play and I've trained as a teacher of music.'

The girl looked round at that, interest flickering in her eyes. Once more she smiled, then nodded shyly and fled.

'That's the first time I've known her to talk to a complete stranger since she came here from the hospital,' said Bertha as she poured coffee. 'The accident shocked her greatly. Has Max told you about it?'

'A little,' replied Lee cautiously, as she took the proffered cup and saucer and sat down beside Bertha on the Chesterfield.

'And that means scarcely anything,' commented Bertha dryly. 'One of Max's great qualities is loyalty to the members of his family, but sometimes I think he carries it a little too far.'

'In what way?'

'He will not admit to any of us having any faults, and that was the case over Bruno. I don't suppose he told you that Bruno was drunk when he was driving Julie up here for the weekend? He divorced Julie's mother some years ago for desertion. He was always a very temperamental person, and since his divorce he hadn't behaved in a very stable way. He had been to some sort of party, decided to come here, and set off when he should have gone to bed and slept it off. The car hit the shoulder of the road and overturned. Bruno was killed instantly, but Julie received concussion and that awful gash on her face.'

'Poor child,' sympathised Lee, recalling her own reaction when learning that her father had been killed. 'No wonder she's shocked!'

Bertha's lined, tanned face creased and her grey eyes twinkled as she smiled.

'I'm amused to hear you say "poor child". To me you look very little more than a child yourself. To tell the truth I'm surprised to see you with someone as hardened and as experienced as Max. I hope he didn't bully you into marrying him.'

Now, how should she answer that? thought Lee as she sipped more of the delicious coffee. Bertha was probing, gently and delicately it was true, but she was definitely trying to find out more about her nephew's hasty marriage.

'Does he always like to get his own way?' she asked. Bertha laughed and clapped her hands together in delight.

'I can see you have the measure of him already. Yes, he does like his own way, and will get it even if it means using devious methods at times. In that way he is very much his father's son. But there were times when he was a boy when he didn't get his own way. He was refused many of the things he asked for, and I suspect it was that more than anything which has made him all the more determined to get what he wants now.'

'Who refused him?' Lee asked incredulously.

'Vincent. He's always been a very strict father, even with Bruno and Irene, but with Max he was more strict because for many years he resented him.'

'Why?'

'Because Carlotta, his wife, died giving birth to the boy, and Vincent worshipped Carlotta.'

Lee's gaze strayed to the guitar which hung on the wall.

'She was from South America?' she queried.

'Yes, from Venezuela. She was three parts Spanish and the other part Indian. I remember when Vincent first brought her home to meet my parents—we were all a little shocked. We were all solid and fair, taking after our Dutch father and English mother, but Carlotta was dark, with beautiful black curls, flashing black eyes and a lovely figure. And besides that, she had nothing to do with trade or business of any sort. She was a singer, temperamental, full of laughter and gaiety one minute and crying as if her heart would break the next. We all loved her, we couldn't help ourselves, and Vincent loved her most of all.' Bertha sighed sadly. 'He was never the same after she died. He retreated into himself. The business became his sole pre-occupation.'

'Poor Max,' Lee said in a spontaneous surge of compassion for the boy she hadn't known. At least she had had her mother for twelve years of her life and her father had continued to love her and take an interest in her. Max, it would seem, for all the wealth which had surrounded him, had had nothing.

'You're the first person I've ever heard say that,' said Bertha. 'Everyone always said "Poor Vincent" or "Poor Carlotta". But you're quite right. Max was the one who suffered, although I think he would be the first to disclaim that he suffered. Love was lacking in his boyhood. He was brought up by a series of nursemaids until he was sent away to school. I didn't live here then—I married a Frenchman and we lived on Martinique. We didn't have any children of our own and several times I asked Vincent if he would let me have Max to live with us, but he always refused.'

'Did he give a reason for refusing?'

'Not Vincent,' said Bertha with her mischievous twinkle. 'You'll see, he's a law unto himself, and he doesn't give reasons. I think he guessed that Max might have been happy with me and François, and he didn't think he should be happy. He thought he should suffer always for being alive when Carlotta was dead. Even now he is still trying to punish Max and that's why ...' Aunt Bertha frowned and gave Lee a wary glance, obviously checking herself as she was about to reveal a family secret. 'No,' she continued as she poured more coffee, 'Max has never been the favourite. Bruno was always that, and it was he who took over the business when Vincent's health broke down, even though everyone knew that Max is the man of business. He's even more astute than his father, although he's clever enough not to let Vincent know that. Actually they get on very well together now, and I know Max would do anything to spare his father pain or suffering of any sort.'

Bertha paused again and it seemed to Lee that the grey glance searched her face for reaction to this remark. Max would do anything, even marry in haste a young woman unknown to the family, so that his father could die happy. That was the implication, she felt sure.

'They're coming now. I can hear the squeak of the wheelchair,' said Bertha quickly. Her eyes twinkled with amusement again. 'You're honoured, my dear. The old lion has condescended to leave his den to come and meet you.'

The wheelchair appeared in the archway. It was pushed by Max. In it sat a man of about seventy-five. He had sparse white hair and a neatly-trimmed white beard and moustache, and although he was very thin his shoulders were square and straight against the back of the chair. Yellowish-coloured skin stretched taut over the bones of his face, giving him a fragile look, but his grey eyes were shrewd and lively amongst the many wrinkles which surrounded them. He was wearing a dark maroon brocade smoking jacket over a white shirt and dark trousers.

'Do you think you should be out of bed, Vincent?' asked Bertha in her calm way.

'I do,' he replied in a surprisingly firm and loud voice. 'I'm damned if I'll receive Max's wife from a sick-bed. Now where is she?'

Lee rose to her feet and went over to him, holding out her hand.

'I'm here, Mr Van Breedan. How are you?' she said nervously. He was really quite intimidating, for all his frailty.

'I've felt better, young woman, but it's kind of you to ask. I can't see you properly, you have your back to the light. Go and sit in that corner of the chesterfield. Max, wheel this thing so that it's beside the arm, next to her. That's right. Good, good. The light falls just where I want it.'

He turned to Lee, leaning over the padded arm of the chesterfield, and before she could move he reached out and grasped her chin. Lifting a monocle which hung on a black riband round his neck, he placed it in his left eye and proceeded to examine her face closely, turning it this way and that.

Mute but mutinous under his intent scrutiny, Lee clenched her fingers in her lap to prevent herself from jerking her head away. She felt as she had felt when Max had stroked his finger down her face two days ago at their first meeting, like a piece of merchandise being appraised before it was purchased. She could hear the rise and fall of Max's and Bertha's voices as they talked, and her nose itched suddenly in reaction to the scent of cigar smoke.

'Will she do?' Max's voice, deep and crisp, put an end to the scrutiny. To her relief Vincent released her and let the monocle fall from his eye. He leaned back and looked at Max who had removed his jacket and loosened his tie, and was lounging in an armchair, smoking.

'Exquisite,' murmured the old man. 'Delicate-looking yet strong, fine lines and excellent colouring. Like a piece of the finest English porcelain china.'

'Now, Vincent, you're talking about Lee as if she were a bargain Max had picked up somewhere,' objected Bertha, giving Lee a conspiratorial wink, and Max laughed, that wicked chuckle which made his face light up with devilry.

'My bargain bride,' he said softly, his eyes glinting as they met Lee's furious glance across the room.

'Marriage isn't a matter of bargain-hunting,' went on Aunt Bertha as if he hadn't spoken.

'I disagree,' replied Vincent urbanely. 'It is. Some people get good bargains, others get bad. If more people applied the techniques of the market place when they're choosing a mate, there might be fewer mistakes made. I compliment you on your choice, *meneer*. So far I can find no fault with

71

her appearance. Aha!' Now it was his turn to chuckle. 'I caught a flash of anger in those big amber eyes. You're a little angry, young woman, because we discuss you in this way. I'm glad, because if you accepted all that we say without objection I'd begin to think you have no spirit, and that would be bad considering the quality of the man you have married. You'd like to tell us all to go to hell, wouldn't you?'

'Yes, I would,' cried Lee, unable to keep her anger under control any longer.

He smiled indulgently and reached out a thin blue-veined hand to touch her head gently.

'Red hair denotes a temper, Max, I hope you realise that!'

'It had crossed my mind,' replied Max dryly, blowing out smoke and grinning at Lee through its haze as she glared at him again. 'Have patience, young one,' he cautioned her, 'the agony will soon be over. You can let go your temper at me, later, when we're alone.'

There was a slow suggestiveness in the way he spoke which hinted that their relationship was closer than it was, intimate, possibly exciting, and Lee was reminded that outwardly their marriage was to appear normal.

'Max tells me you can play the guitar,' said Vincent. 'Could you play that one which is hanging on the wall? It would give me great pleasure if you could.'

How could she refuse? She didn't really want to refuse. She had been longing to play the guitar ever since she had seen it. She glanced at Max. Imperceptibly he nodded his head.

'I expect it needs tuning,' she said.

'So you will tune it now,' replied the autocratic old man. 'Then you will sing a song to me, one you like well.'

He sighed and leaned his head back as if he were very tired, and her irritation evaporated at once. Rising to her feet, she went over and lifted the guitar down, smiling a little at the bunches of gay ribbons, now a little faded and dusty, which decorated it. Carrying it back to her seat, she rested it across her knees and began to tune the strings, plucking each one and adjusting its tautness with the ebony keys. Soon she was totally engrossed in what she was doing and took no more interest in the conversation which was going on between the others.

When the instrument was tuned to her satisfaction, she played a few testing chords and then began to hum a little Brazilian song of which she was very fond.

'*Azulao*. The Bluebird, by Ovalle,' murmured the old man. 'One of Carlotta's favourites too, even though it was not from her country. Sing it, please.'

Lee glanced at him in surprise. The song was a light gay one strongly reflecting the folk elements found in Brazilian music, and she had often sung it at the club in Amsterdam. The lyrics were supposedly sung by a lover to the bluebird asking it to fly to his beloved to tell her that his life without her was worthless. In a way, she supposed, it could describe Vincent Van Breedan's feelings since his wife had died some thirty-odd years ago. Life without his Carlotta had been worthless to him.

Softly she began to sing, a little self-conscious at first because she was having to sing alone before a small but attentive audience, but gradually growing more confident as the gay melody with its strong beat swept her along and the pure sweet sound of her voice soared up.

When she had finished there was a short silence. Then Bertha clapped her hands together and exclaimed:

'Bravo, bravo, child! That was lovely. Do you know the song about the hunter? *O Cacaor*, I think it's called, and it's also from Brazil. The hunter is so caught up in the web of love that he goes hunting without his gun. Carlotta used to sing that too.'

73

'Yes, I do,' said Lee.

'Play it,' ordered Vincent gruffly.

Lee looked across to the chair where Max had been sitting and quivered with surprise. He had gone. He was nowhere in the room. She hadn't noticed him going, and she felt a curious jolt of disappointment because he had not stayed to hear her sing the next song.

This time when she finished singing Vincent reached out and took one of her hands in both of his.

'You have a sweet voice, my dear, and you play the guitar admirably. You have made me very happy this morning and I hope you and Max will stay here for a few days, so that I can hear you play again. I know it is your honeymoon and perhaps you would have liked to have gone away somewhere by yourselves—but you can be alone at the beach house and yet be on hand to dance attendance on a selfish old man. Later, when you and I have got to know one another a little better, he can take you away, perhaps to Aruba.'

'That's right,' agreed Bertha. 'Irene, Max's elder sister, lives there. She will want to meet you too. Shall I get Josh to come and take you back to your room, Vincent?'

'If you please,' said the old man. His eyes were closed and he looked very frail. Bertha beckoned to Lee, who placed the guitar on the wall and followed the older woman from the room, almost colliding with the dark-faced man in hospital white who was about to enter and who, she assumed, was Vincent's nurse.

'Max has gone down to the beach,' said Aunt Bertha. 'I'll walk down with you, to show you the way.'

A path wound through tangled green foliage which clothed the sloping cliffside and ended at a clearing in which a simple wooden bungalow had been built. Below the building, a crescent of fine white sand rimmed a small bay of sparkling greenish-blue water. On the shore a var-

74

nished sailing dinghy with a high raking mast was beached and beside it stood Max, already changed into brief black shorts and simple cotton T-shirt.

As they approached him Aunt Bertha said casually,

'Did you know you're married to a champion dinghy racer, Lee?'

'No, I didn't,' replied Lee unthinkingly, then could have bitten her tongue out as Bertha gave her a sharp sidelong glance. If their relationship had been close, Max would have told her about his favourite form of recreation.

'He's very uncommunicative,' she said lightly, smiling at him and daringly tucking her hand through his arm. 'Getting him to talk about himself is like trying to prise open an oyster's shell.'

'So you've found that out too,' said Bertha, nodding, her eyes gleaming with admiration as well as amusement, and the difficult moment passed. 'For today I'll get Emma to bring your lunch down to you, but for other days you can prepare it yourselves, and other meals too. There's plenty of food stocked in the place. We shall, of course, expect you to come and have dinner with us, but not tonight. You'll want to be alone, quite naturally. All right, Max?'

'All right, Aunt Bertha,' he replied with a grin. 'You seem to have everything well organised as usual. We'll see you tomorrow.'

'Yes, but Max, do be careful,' she warned, looking a little anxious. 'If you take Lee sailing with you try not to capsize. It might put her off wanting to go out altogether, and that would be a shame.'

'Yes, Aunty,' he replied with a wicked glint in his eyes. 'I'll be careful.'

Aunt Bertha went off and Lee withdrew her arm from Max's to turn and look at the dinghy. It had smooth sleek lines and seemed to be full of ropes and gadgets for which she had no names. A white sail billowed out of a blue bag, and beside it were long thin flat pieces of wood about an inch and a half wide. Max picked one of them up and began to push it into a pocket sewn on the side of the sail.

'Is it true, are you a champion dinghy sailor?' Lee asked, turning to look at him. She was holding her wide-brimmed picture hat in her hand, and the wind belled out the full skirt of her dress and pulled her hair sideways across her face and the back of her head so that the shining copper-tinted stuff bunched all at one side.

'That's why I was in England last year, to take part in the international meeting for this class of dinghy. Later I sailed in Holland too,' he replied coolly.

'You should have told me. Aunt Bertha seemed surprised that I didn't know.'

'Yes, I suppose I should,' he murmured as he shoved another of the long flat pieces of wood into another pocket. 'Would knowing that I sail have made any difference otherwise?'

'Difference to what?' she asked.

'Our relationship. Would you have married me if I'd opened up and told you that you'd have to share me with a racing dinghy while we're on our honeymoon?'

He was mocking her for what she had said about him being like an oyster.

'If you want to spend your spare time sailing that's your affair, and has nothing to do with me!' she retorted rather weakly.

'So you don't want to come with me this afternoon. You'd prefer to curl up on your bed for a siesta, perhaps to dream about Hartog, and what might have been,' he taunted.

Go with him! The suggestion overrode the jeer about Adrian. She looked at the gleaming boat, saw herself in it as she had seen others, leaning out over the side to keep it upright as it skimmed over the glittering waves, and with

76

every fibre of her being she longed to go with him.

'Could I?' she asked hopefully. 'I've never been in a sailing boat before, but I've often longed to sail. I used to go and watch them sailing in Holland last summer. I might have watched you, for all we know.'

'Yes, you might, mightn't you?' he said, turning his head to look at her, amusement gleaming in his eyes. 'Yes, you could come with me, provided you won't mind being yelled at when you do something wrong or aren't quick enough— and don't mind getting soaked to the skin by flying spray or having your hands blistered by rope. You could come.'

For a moment time was suspended as Lee looked up and met his intent gaze. She felt strongly, instinctively, that the moment was important and that any decision she made now was going to count as much in her life, if not more, than the one she had made when she had decided to marry him. Youthful enthusiasm for doing something new and which, until now, had not been possible made it easy for her to decide.

'I'd like to go with you, if you'll tell me what to do,' she said earnestly, and saw his eyebrows go up.

'You never cease to surprise me,' he murmured. 'Good! Let's go in. I've put your case and your guitar inside. Change into shorts or pants and a shirt, anything you don't mind getting wet; you'll have to tie up your hair too, or it might get tangled in something. By the time you're changed, lunch should be here.'

She went after him up the steps which led from the beach to the wooden verandah. A screen door opened into a long room running the width of the house, with wide windows overlooking the sea. Its walls were panelled in golden wood and the furniture was upholstered in green linen-type material which had also been used for the window curtains. At one end there was a dining table set about with four chairs.

Doorways at the back of the room led into the kitchen, the bathroom and into a room with a big double bed. Max pointed to Lee's case, which he had placed at the end of the bed. He caught her enquiring glance as they left the room and answered the drift of her thoughts.

'There's another room, behind the kitchen. I'll sleep in there,' he said casually. 'Now you change while I set the table for lunch.'

Three hours later Lee stood before the long mirror in the bedroom of the bungalow and surveyed her appearance with a rueful grin. Her face was sunburnt, her hair was a tangle, her bare legs were bleached with dried salt water, and her brief clothing, shorts and cotton blouse, was soaked. Holding out her hands, she looked at them with more concern. There were blisters on the soft pads below each finger, and some of them had broken to reveal raw red skin beneath.

But it had been worth it, she thought as she grabbed a towel and padded out of the room on bare feet to the bathroom. That time spent with Max in the sailing dinghy had been one of the most exhilarating in her life. The little boat had surged across the waves, pulled onwards by big mainsail and smaller foresail. At first she had crouched on the thwart under the boom, then at a brisk order from Max she had moved to the side if the boat as it had tipped over, and finally she had found herself leaning out, hanging on with her toes beneath a toe strap, doing her best to be horizontal to counteract the weight of the wind in the sail.

Another sharp, shouted order and she was having to duck in again under the boom because, in the shelter of the cliffs, the wind was not so strong and the boat didn't lean over so much. In, then out again, flinging herself desperately backwards, clinging with feet and knees, holding on to the rope of the foresail.

An hour full of speed and action, of co-ordination between mind and body and crowded with new images. Max
with his eyes covered by sun-glasses, his mouth a straight
determined line, his dark hair ruffled above his broad brow;
sitting out with her, muscles flexed in his bare, sun-tanned
arm as he steered the dinghy. The swish of water under the
hull, the gurgle of it under the bow, the sudden hissing of it
as the bow came up the boat had steadied temporarily, and
Max had shouted triumphantly, 'We're planing!' as if that
was his most desired ambition.

Lee stepped out of her clothing, stepped into the bath,
pulled the shower curtain round and turned on the taps,
tested the heat of the water and pressed the lever which
would start the shower. She would go again even if it meant
blistering her fingers, those fingers of which until now she
had taken the greatest care because they had to pluck the
strings of a guitar. She would go again because she had
loved every minute of the time she had been out there,
feeling as if she were a part of the sea and the sky. And
everyone would think she was doing it because she wanted
to be with Max, and had married him because she loved
him.

Out of the bath she dried herself in a leisurely fashion,
squeezing water out of her hair and shaking it back behind
her shoulders. She caught sight of her face, glowing pink,
and laughed·at her reflection. If she wasn't careful she
would become lobster-coloured!

A banging on the door startled her, reminding her that
she was not alone in this house, would never be alone in it
because she was sharing it with Max.

'Hurry up!' he called through the door.

Quickly she draped the big towel round her, picked up
her wet clothing, opened the door and stepped forward,
only to retreat into the bathroom again. He was right outside, bare to his middle, still wearing his wet shorts, a big

muscular man whose bronzed skin gleamed, whose black hair curled damply and whose sharp grey eyes glinted with interest as they noted her bare shoulders and the slipping towel.

He put out a finger and touched her wind-burned cheek.

'The delicate porcelain could get damaged by too much sun. We must take care of it. Next time use a stronger lotion to protect your skin.' His hand dropped to his side and the corner of his mouth lifted in a sardonic smile as she retreated even further from him. 'You made a hit with Vincent this morning, as I guessed you might, and I wouldn't want it any other way. He judges all women by one standard—my mother.'

'Aunt Bertha told me a little about her,' said Lee, coming forward again inching past him, one hand clutching the towel to her bosom, the other one dangling her shorts and shirt. 'She must have been a lively and interesting person to live with.'

The big shoulders shrugged.

'I've only other people's word for that,' he replied coldly. 'You probably sing better than she did because you've been trained properly, but it was the fact that you can play and sing a song she used to sing, more than anything else, which made my father accept you this morning. I didn't even have to show him the marriage certificate.'

She couldn't quite make it into the passageway without brushing against him—and that was something she did not want to risk, body contact. There would be other meetings like this during the next week or two, she realised with an inner shakiness. In this small house they could not avoid running into one another, and she would have to take more care how she dressed.

Caught between the door jamb and him she leaned back, trying to be casual.

'And now I suppose you're going to tell me you asked

me to marry you because you knew I could play and sing that type of song,' she accused lightly.

His smile was a white tantalising flash and she felt her heart leap in her breast in reaction to his sudden overwhelming attraction. The smile added another facet to his personality, just as the sailing had done.

'I have to admit it tipped the scales in your favour considerably,' he drawled. 'I think I did a good day's work today. I picked a good bargain when I married you.'

Mockery was dancing in his eyes, robbing them of their customary coldness. It softened his deep voice to a caressing murmur as, placing a hand above her on the door jamb, he leaned over her in an attitude which shrieked to her of passion. She felt trapped in more ways than one. Stiffening against the wooden upright, feeling it dig into her back, clutching the slipping towel against her in a desperate hand, she lifted her chin and retorted:

'Possibly you'll get more than you bargained for!'

That seemed to amuse him, for his mouth curved again. His head tipped forward and once again his thick black lashes made fans which screened effectively the expression in his eyes as he seemed to appraise the ivory-tinted curves of her bare shoulders. Still she could not get past him, and the trapped feeling was making her heart hammer with panic.

But he did not touch her. Instead he looked up again and his sharp bright glance pinned her down, so that she felt like a butterfly which has been caught and pinned down by a lepidopterist so that it can be studied more closely.

'If I do get more than I bargained for it will be for the first time in my life,' he replied enigmatically, and straightening up he turned into the bathroom, closing the door behind him before Lee had a chance to retort.

Breath came out of her in a gusty sigh. Relief was mixed with a feeling of anticlimax as she padded back to the safety

81

of the bedroom and closed the door. Living with an enigma was going to be exhausting in spite of the rules that governed their relationship, for there was always the possibility that he might decide to break those rules—and no matter what sort of resistance she might be able to offer, she had an instinctive feeling it would not be strong enough to prevent him from having his own way.

CHAPTER FOUR

FOOTSTEPS sounded on the wooden steps which led up to the door of the beach bungalow. The door opened, then slammed shut as if pulled by an angry hand. In the kitchen where she was preparing a salad for the midday meal, Lee stiffened involuntarily and glanced sideways to the doorway of the room. A green pepper in one hand and a chopping knife in the other, she waited tensely for Max to appear.

He did not come. She heard the bathroom door open and shut, then the noise of water running from a tap. At once tension oozed out of her and she sagged in reaction, closing her eyes in relief.

She and Max had been married for almost two weeks. The days had passed by slowly, sunny and serene, each one having the quality of a pleasant dream; a dream which was taking place in a beautiful location in a tropical paradise where sparkling white sand rimmed a cove of greenish-blue water and stiff-leaved palms dropped gracefully over the shore.

Every morning she wakened to the smell of coffee being made in the kitchen by Max. Every morning she got up and went to join him to share breakfast with him, sitting out on the verandah to listen to the lap of water on the sand and the rustle of the wind in the trees, to watch the glitter of morning sunlight on the waves of the blue sea.

After breakfast they sailed in the dinghy, returning to have their lunch together. After lunch they went their separate ways. Usually she went to her room to rest because she was not yet accustomed to the heat of the midday, but where Max went during that time she did not know. Later in the afternoon they either swam or sunbathed or he would take her to visit another part of the island. Many times they went up to the old house to visit his father, Bertha and Juliana, to join friends and relatives who had heard of Max's hasty marriage and had called to meet his bride.

Lee found it easy to be a wife in name only when there were other people about. In company she forgot she was not a wife in the fullest sense of the word; the part of Mrs Max Van Breedan came to her naturally in public, and so far she had been able to accept the congratulations which had been offered without any awkwardness.

The part of being an interested and concerned daughter-in-law of Vincent Van Breedan had not given her any difficulties either. She liked the old man and enjoyed playing and singing to him. He was blunt and forthright, but he was also kind, and in her state of disillusionment after the way Adrian had let her down, she craved kindness. Aunt Bertha, too, provided a calm and often humorous motherliness which Lee had found lacking in her life.

With Juliana she was making progress. After offering to teach the girl how to play the guitar, she had asked Vincent if his grandchild might have the use of his dead wife's guitar. He had agreed, and now Juliana had been coming for the past few days, after siesta time, to learn how to play chords and simple accompaniments.

In giving the lessons Lee felt she was doing some good, making in her own way a contribution to the rehabilitation of the girl, in return for the shelter and keep which being Max's wife gave her.

Yes, really the time had passed very pleasantly. Yet she was aware of strange disturbances within herself, and after thinking about them she had come to the conclusion that they were the result of the time she had to spend alone with Max.

He seemed to have no difficulty in sloughing, like an extra skin, the part he played in public as her husband. When they were alone he treated her as coolly as he had always done. She, on the other hand, was often strung-up and ill at ease when they were alone—especially when they sat together in the evenings on the verandah watching the bright stars flower in the velvety blackness of the sky. Then tension would make her tongue-tied. Usually she tried to ease it by playing her guitar. Whether he liked her playing or not she did not know, because he never made any comment.

And also, every evening, she would wonder a little dismally what she might have been doing if she had been married to Adrian instead of Max. The answer to such wonderings only made her more uncomfortable, so that she would excuse herself and go to her room to sit there alone until it was time to go to bed.

Only when they went sailing did she seem to get close to Max, and she looked forward to the times when they pushed the dinghy off the beach, the sails filled and the boat danced across the water. While helping him to sail it she forgot to be concerned about their relationship, and as a result found herself in close communion with him.

But this morning the feeling had come so close to a sensation of joy that she had been frightened, and when they had returned to the beach and Max had turned to her and said casually, 'You're fast becoming one of the best crews I've ever had,' she had been so stunned by the pleasure his praise had given her that she had been unable to stay near him a minute longer in case she had shown him she was glad he enjoyed sailing with her as much as she did with him, and she had turned to run away from him across the sparkling sand, to hide from him in the bungalow. He had not followed her at once, staying to finish putting away the sails as usual, but she knew that when he did come in he would be full of questions about her erratic behaviour.

'Aren't you going to finish dicing that pepper?'

He spoke from the doorway, amusement quivering in his voice. Lee jumped in reaction and glanced at him. She sensed he was often amused by her, and the knowledge that he was made her feel very young and inexperienced. Now he was leaning against the jamb of the doorway, his arms folded across his chest, his head tipped forward as he surveyed her from under his strangely-peaked dark eyebrows. A damp cotton T-shirt clung to his muscular chest and brief white shorts set off his tanned, thewed thighs; and, as always when he had been sailing, his raven-black hair curled riotously over his head.

His physical appearance gave her a jolt, making her incapable of speech or movement, so that she could only stare at him.

'You're very pale,' he said. 'Have you got a touch of the sun?'

He often showed concern for her health and her appearance, as if he didn't want his bargain to show signs of wear and tear.

'No, you gave me a fright. I didn't hear you come in here.'

'So I'd noticed. I've been standing here for about three minutes,' he replied.

Disconcerted, Lee finished chopping the pepper rapidly and nervously. Then she added the green dices to the salad, lifted up the bowl and said as calmly as she could,

'Lunch is ready now. What would you like to drink? Beer or coffee?'

'Beer. I'll get it.'

At the table she watched him covertly, waiting for him to question her about her impulsive flight from the beach. Usually she stayed to help him put the sails away and leave the dinghy ship-shape ready for the next sail, so he was bound to ask why she had run away, and she had no slick explanation prepared, nothing that would deceive that shrewd mind of his.

The beer gurgled in a golden stream as he poured it into a tall stein. White foam frothed on the top, glittering as it reflected the sunlight which shafted through the slats of the shutters, already closed over the windows to keep out the hot brilliance. Lee stared at the foam watching it disappear slowly as it was absorbed into the golden liquid below it. Then a big hand grasped the handle of the stein and it was lifted upwards, so she turned her attention to heaping salad on to her plate.

'Did you hurt yourself when we were sailing today?' asked Max when he had also helped himself to salad.

'No, I didn't,' she replied coolly, not looking at him as she put more salad in her mouth and savoured the crunchiness and freshness of the vegetables and fruits from which it had been made.

'Then what's wrong?'

'Nothing.'

'Try again, Lee,' he ordered quietly, and she felt a quiver of alarm as she always did when he wasn't satisfied with any of her answers. 'Why didn't you stay to help me put the boat away?'

'Just because I didn't help you put the boat away it doesn't mean there's anything wrong,' she parried. 'Do I have to help you put things away? Is it part of my job as your wife?'

He gave her a sharp underbrowed glance and his mouth curled unpleasantly at one corner, a sure sign that he was irritated by the uncharacteristic sting in her reply.

'Do you consider sailing with me as part of your job as my wife?' he countered. 'My impression is otherwise. I think you come because you enjoy it.' He waited for that thrust to go home, then added more gently, 'I was asking

87

you why you didn't stay to help because you seem upset about something, and I thought perhaps I'd done something to upset you.'

She felt rebuked and flushed to the roots of her hair, immediately hating him because he had the power to make her feel that way.

'I'm sorry,' she mumbled, 'but honestly, Max, there's nothing wrong. Nothing I can tell you, that is,' she faltered as his eyes expressed their disbelief in one lightning-flash of a glance.

'That means I *am* to blame. Come on, tell me. What have I done? If we're going to continue to live together, we have to be honest with each other. I don't believe in your "honestly".'

Confused, she searched her mind for something to say to put him off, although she knew from recent experience that it would be difficult. Persistence was his second name.

'I can't tell you. Please don't make me,' she pleaded.

He leaned back in his chair and laughed.

'How shall I *make* you?' he challenged. 'Put you on the rack? Turn the thumbscrews? Inject a truth serum?'

'Juliana says you can make anyone do anything you want, and Aunt Bertha told me once that you always get your own way, even if you have to use devious methods sometimes,' Lee said, hoping to make him desist from asking more questions by diverting him into defence of himself against such accusations. But he merely raised his eyebrows in mockery and was not at all diverted.

'I see that you're not going to tell me, so I'll have to use one of those devious methods you refer to,' he replied smoothly, leaning forward with his folded arms on the table so that he could pin her down with his dagger-sharp eyes. 'Let me think what's happened so far today. Nothing went wrong at breakfast time, I ate everything you put before me. Nothing happened after breakfast. I was a dutiful husband

88

and helped you clear the table. Afterwards I made my own bed, picked up my dirty clothing and put it in the clothes basket. On the way to the dinghy *I* carried the sail bags, battens and other equipment. *You* carried nothing. When we were out sailing I didn't shout at you once, even though you were a little slow at getting the foresail in a couple of times. When we returned ...' He broke off in the middle of his satirical account of their morning together as he noted the rise of colour in her cheek. 'I see,' he said softly, 'I seem to have offended you by praising you and telling you you're becoming a good crew. I shall have to be more careful in the future about what I say.'

'Oh! Oh, you ... I ... it's impossible to keep anything from you,' she blurted. 'I can't explain why I behaved as I did. I just found I couldn't bear to be with you a minute longer.'

'Does that happen often?' His eyes were narrowed to gleaming slits.

'Yes.' She whispered the word, looking at him with an expression of fear in her golden eyes; fear because she did not wish to hurt his feelings. Then she remembered he had no feelings to hurt. Inside he was made of ice.

'I'm all right when there are other people about,' she hurried to explain, 'when we're having to pretend our marriage is normal. It's when we're alone ...'

She couldn't continue because she didn't know how. Her feelings about him were too confused for expression. How could you put into words a jumble of fear, respect, near-hate and longing?

'When we're alone you're very much aware that our marriage is not normal,' he finished for her dryly. 'And that makes you feel uncomfortable?'

She nodded, and then at once wished she hadn't agreed with him. Now he would think she never enjoyed his company, which wasn't true. Contrarily she blamed him for having put her into a position of agreeing with him, because he was so cool and calculating about it all, analysing the situation as if he were doing market research in preparation for launching the sale of a new product.

'Oh, can't you be less businesslike about everything and show more feeling?' she blurted out of her confusion. 'If only you would behave more like a human being instead of like a business machine!'

Her outburst seemed to hang like an echo in the warm sun-shot dimness of the room. Minutes passed in silence as they measured glances across the table.

'Are you sure you mean that?' Max queried at last. 'Ours is a business arrangement, and perhaps I should remind you that you agreed to marry me after certain conditions were laid down. One in particular seemed to be very important to you. Now I'm sure you wouldn't like it if I disregarded the discipline imposed upon us both by that condition and behaved as a husband does in a normal marriage, especially when on his honeymoon.'

The crisp iciness of his voice chilled her. As the heat of her confusion died down she retreated at once, avoiding his glance, feeling her cheeks glow.

'That isn't what I meant,' she said stiffly.

'Then what did you mean?' he demanded relentlessly.

'I wish you'd tell me what you feel instead of always thinking before you speak,' she said, looking up again.

He leaned back from the table, and to her relief she saw humour gleam elusively in his eyes.

'How like you to want to change the leopard's spots,' he taunted quietly. 'All right, I'll have a go at doing what you ask. What do you want me to tell you my feelings about?'

She wanted to know how he felt after two weeks of marriage to her; how he felt about living in the same house, of sharing everything except a bedroom. But all she could get out, rather lamely, was:

'Do you feel uncomfortable when we're alone together?'

His fingers curled round the handle of the stein and he looked down at the remainder of the beer. His eyes were hidden so that his face had that dark, devilish, secretive appearance. He was thinking again before he spoke, and that wasn't what she wanted.

'Max!' she pleaded, and he glanced up sharply.

'No, I don't feel uncomfortable when we're alone together. I like it, but then I'm not forever imagining what it would be like to be married to someone else, as you are always doing,' he said, and raising the stein he drained it.

Lee should have remembered he was good at knife-thrusts, she thought as pain stabbed through her. He was good at guessing what went on in her mind, too.

'There is a remedy for your discomfort,' he said, pushing his chair back from the table and rising to his feet.

'What is it?' she quavered, beginning to collect up dirty dishes. Lunch was over. It was siesta time, although she did not take a long rest because Julie came for her lesson in the afternoon.

'Spend less time alone together,' he replied, going over to the settee where her guitar was lying. As he sat down the instrument twanged and he picked it up to hold it across his knee and pluck idly at the strings.

'Is that possible?' she asked.

'Now that I've done what I wanted to do, shown to Vincent that I'm married to the sort of woman he wanted me to marry, we can get out of here and spend the last week of our so-called honeymoon in Aruba, stay in a luxury hotel and live it up. There would be plenty of entertainment. You could dance all night if you wanted. Would you like that?'

He was offering her sweets again, as they might be offered to a child who was suffering from boredom and frustration. Lee resented the implication, but had to admit she would like to dance and see some bright lights.

91

'Would you?' she ventured.

He looked across at her and grinned.

'Oh, I enjoy the high life as much as the next person,' he drawled. 'And it might be interesting showing it to an innocent like you, watching those big amber eyes widen with shock, seeing that nose wrinkle with distaste.'

'Why do you assume I'd be shocked or feel distaste?' she countered. 'I might like it! I might do more than dance. I might lead you a dance.'

He considered her in that slow appraising way he had which always roused her temper.

'I'd like to see you try,' he murmured enigmatically, and turned his attention to the guitar, beginning to tune it, much to her surprise. 'Have you ever played blackjack or roulette?' he inquired.

'No, I've never had enough money to gamble.'

'How wise of you,' he mocked. 'Then I shall stake you and watch you run the gamut of emotions as the dealer calls his number or the wheel turns. And there'll be all the people you can ever want around you, because it will be carnival time.'

He played a few chords and then to her astonishment began to play a haunting little French tune called *Romance d'Amour*, which she knew only too well. Its bitter-sweet melody might have roused nostalgia for Adrian if she had not been so amazed by this new aspect of the man she had married. His playing was clear and accurate if a little cold. There was no fumbling or hesitation. He played the instrument as he sailed the boat, with the maximum of concentration, intent on achieving perfection.

'I didn't know you could play,' she said, putting down the dishes she had been holding and going over to sit on the leather-covered pouffe which was at his feet beside the settee. 'Your father told me that none of his children are musical.'

'He meant in comparison with his wife,' he replied with a touch of dryness. 'Bruno was the best, but then he was taught by my mother. Irene, too, can perform adequately. I taught myself on the guitar that Juliana is playing, in secret. It came naturally.'

Lee sat, elbow on knee, hand under chin, listening, watching the big tanned hands move skilfully up and down the strings, imagining him as a boy, wilful and determined, teaching himself to play the instrument in the secrecy of his room in the old *landhuis*. She felt compassion for that boy who had been denied the interest and affection which his brother and sister had received, because his mother had died at his birth.

'You should have told me you can play,' she said softly, speaking out of that feeling of compassion. She was always looking for ways to crack the ice.

'Why should I have told you?' he countered. 'If I'd told you everything about myself before we got married there would be nothing for you to discover, and I'm told that marriage is one long voyage of discovery of which the honeymoon is only the reconnaissance period.'

The haunting melody came to its quiet ending and he struck a mocking dissonant chord which was completely out of keeping with the romantic mood of the tune. The chord seemed to underline the irony with which he spoke and reminded Lee once again that theirs was not a normal marriage and might come to an end once Vincent died.

Max put the guitar aside and leaned forward. His movement brought him very close to her where she sat crouched on the pouffe, but for once she did not move away.

'You seem surprised by my ability to play the guitar,' he scoffed.

'I am. Like the sailing, it changes the image I had of you.'

'The image of the businessman who thinks before he speaks, you mean?' he asked.

'Yes. Is it an image?' she said hopefully.

'No, it isn't. It's the real me, but so are the sailing and guitar-playing and other recreations which I pursue. They are expressions of the entity which is me.'

Head down, the curtain of her copper-silk hair sliding forward to half-hide her face, Lee thought about what Max had just said. The touch of his hand against her chin came as a fresh, nerve-tingling surprise. He had not touched her when they had been alone together since he had kissed her in the quiet sunlit entrance hall of the building where they had been married. Now the weight of his hand forced her to look at him.

He was so close she could see silvery hairs flecking the sideburns which curled down his cheeks, the fine network of lines at the corners of his eyes caused by narrowing them against sun-glare, the hollow blackness of his pupils dilated by the dimness of the room, so that the pale iris was but a faint glimmer of steel-grey.

'You're working too hard at this job of being married,' he said gently. 'Take it as it comes. It's happening to me too, you know. I'm on that voyage of discovery with you. I'm discovering you.'

The moment was delicately balanced, fraught with possibilities. Lee was sure he must be able to hear her heart change gear and beat at a faster pace than was normal. His glance drifted down to her mouth and although her nerves twanged she did not move or go into retreat as the words *take it as it comes* repeated in her mind.

Footsteps, heavy and plodding, sounded on the wooden steps outside. Juliana was coming for her guitar lesson, a little earlier than usual because she was keen. Max's hand fell away, he stood up, and by the time Juliana pushed open the screen door he had gone into the kitchen on his way through to the small room at the back where he slept.

'Is Uncle Max here?' asked Juliana. She was carrying

her grandmother's guitar.

'Yes, he is. Do you want to speak to him?' replied Lee.

She felt all keyed up, her nerves stretched tautly like the strings of her own guitar which Max had tuned so well. What would have happened if Juliana had not come at that moment? Would she ever know what would have happened? Deliberately she tried to calm herself to relax.

Take it as it comes. Remember it's a job. Stop trying to change it into something else. You wouldn't like it if he behaved as a husband in a normal marriage. You wouldn't have liked it if he had kissed you just now and made love to you because you're not in love with him.

'No, not really,' Julie was saying with that frightening Van Breedan honesty, 'but Aunt Bertha said I was to give him a message.'

'What is it?' Max spoke curtly from the kitchen doorway and Juliana gave him a sidelong glance as she sat down on the settee.

'She said I was to tell you that Mrs Volney has come and would like to see you.' Juliana's voice was stilted and she did not look at him while she gave the message. 'There's been a change in the arrangements for the takeover. Mrs Deering has come back.'

Her message delivered, Juliana seemed to become engrossed in tuning her guitar. Watching Max, Lee thought he looked rather exasperated.

'Are you sure she said Mrs Deering?' he queried sharply.

'Yes,' replied the girl colourlessly. 'She made me repeat the message to make sure I got it right. Mrs Deering has come back, that's what she said I was to tell you. Can we start now, Lee? I've been practising and practising, and I think I can play those pieces you gave me yesterday without a mistake.'

The screen door opened and clanged shut. Max had gone. Lee felt the tension ease out of her.

'Lee, are you all right?' Now Juliana's voice was different, warm with concern, and her greenish eyes were dark with anxiety.

'Yes, yes, of course I am.' Lee pushed the hair back from her forehead. It was the climate, she decided. She wasn't used yet to these hot afternoons, and she had missed her siesta.

'You don't look all right. You're awfully pale, and there's a funny look round your eyes. Has Uncle Max been horrid to you?'

'No, he hasn't.' Quite the reverse in fact, she thought.

'I thought he looked very cross and frowny,' said Juliana.

'That's because ...' Lee broke off, caught her lip between her teeth. She had been going to say that Max had probably looked cross because Juliana had come just at an interesting point in his relationship with his wife, but decided that was something she could not say to this teenager. Also she might be deceived by her own imagination. He could have been cross because the message he had received had not pleased him.

'Who is Mrs Deering?' she asked.

Julie's eyes glinted knowingly.

'That's what I thought too,' she said in a gossipy whisper. 'He was cross when he heard she's back. She was his girlfriend years and years ago, but she married another man and went away to live in the United States.'

'How do you know all this?' asked Lee.

'Family talk,' replied Juliana. 'When Aunty Irene comes to visit she and Aunt Bertha talk about Uncle Max all the time. You see he's always had lots of girl-friends, and they were always wondering which one he would marry.'

'Do you know why Mrs Deering is back? Is she visiting relatives?' asked Lee.

'I don't know, but you needn't worry. You're much prettier than she is.'

'How do you know? Have you met her?' Lee was beginning to feel a little irritated by Juliana's sly reference to Max's girl-friends, and the impression she gave of women vying with each other for his favours.

'Yes, once, last year. She came to the house in Willemstad to have dinner with Daddy and me. She said I was to call her Aunty Beatrix and to think of her as a relative, because one day she might be. I didn't believe her. How could she become a relative of mine? Only if she married either Daddy or Uncle Max, and she couldn't do that because she was already married. Can I play to you now?'

The lesson went quite well, and when it was over they went for a swim in the warm buoyant water of the cove. Afterwards they lay on the beach talking.

'I wish you could stay here all the time,' confided Juliana, sitting up suddenly and hugging her knees. 'Having you to talk to has made such a difference for me.'

'But shouldn't you be in school?' asked Lee, raising a subject Max had asked her to discuss with Juliana when she felt the time was favourable.

There was a little silence. Glancing at the girl, she saw the plump face was crumpled with worry, and wished she had never mentioned school.

'I haven't been to school since the accident,' said the girl, jerkily, painfully.

'You should go back, Julie, and finish your education. It would be a shame if you didn't. I've been told you're quite clever.'

'I can't go back,' mumbled the girl, her hand going to the livid, reddish scar which angled across her cheek. 'I couldn't face all those people staring at me. And I'd have to live in Willemstad.'

'That's easy. You could live with your uncle and me,' said Lee, then had a rueful thought. How like her to make an impulsive commitment like that before she had thought it out, before she had consulted Max about it! 'Your father made him your guardian in his will, and I'm sure he wants to do his best for you,' she continued, as much to convince herself as the girl.

'It's not true. He doesn't care about me! He wishes I'd been killed with Daddy,' Julie cried out, hiding her face on her bent knees so that all that could be seen was a tangle of shining sun-shot brown hair.

Lee felt her face go taut and white.

'Julie, that's a terrible thing to say about anyone. I'm sure Max doesn't feel like that about you,' she remonstrated rather feebly.

'He does! I'm a nuisance to him. I'm in his way.'

'Has he ever said so?'

'No.' It was a sullen mutter.

'Then how do you know he feels like that?'

'I just know, that's all.'

'That's a silly answer,' argued Lee patiently. 'You must have heard someone saying something about Max for you to know. Now tell me, so that I can tell you whether it's right.'

Julie raised her head. The expression in her usually dull greenish eyes was almost pitying.

'How can you do that?' she challenged. 'You know nothing about Uncle Max or how he feels about anything. You've only been married to him two weeks. Daddy knew him for years, and he always said he didn't understand him. He said Uncle Max is as close as the devil and never lets anyone know what he's feeling, so how can you know how he feels about me? How can you judge whether what I feel about him is right or not? You're a stranger here and you know nothing.'

It was like a slap in the face and Lee had to acknowledge its truth, but she was in so far now that she had to go on, and try to find out why Juliana felt she was in Max's way and a nuisance to him.

'You could still tell me why you feel the way you do,' she urged gently.

'No, I can't! I won't,' exclaimed Juliana, springing to her feet so that sand spattered over Lee. 'I don't want to talk about it any more. And I don't want to go back to school . . . ever!'

She ran off towards the path. Lee sprang to her feet and called after her.

'Julie, come back! Wait! Please!'

But Juliana went on. Sighing, Lee made her way to the bungalow. With a few unthinking words she had undone all the good she had done. It would take hours of patience and perseverance to reach again the point of confidence which they had reached today. If only she had not mentioned Max to the girl! If only she had not said what she felt to be true, that he wanted to do his best for his niece.

She must hurry and try to catch Juliana before the girl hid away in her room, which was her reaction to anything she disliked. After all, part of the job as Max's wife was to help his ward and try to give her the moral support she needed.

Changing quickly into a dress, she brushed her hair and, picking up Carlotta Van Breedan's guitar, she left the bungalow. All the way up the path she kept hoping to meet Max on his return from the big house so that she could tell him what had happened, but he didn't appear, and there was no sign of him when she reached the house.

Aunt Bertha was there, though, sitting out on the gallery.

'Come here, Lee,' she called. 'Someone would like to meet you.'

Sitting in comfortable chairs beside a small round table on which a tea tray glinted in the sunlight, Aunt Bertha and her companion were sipping tea from delicate china cups.

99

'This is Sophy Volney,' Aunt Bertha introduced the tall plump woman whose china blue eyes surveyed Lee curiously.

'Did you know that you're the talk of the business community?' The woman's voice was loud and harsh and she spoke English with a pronounced guttural accent.

'No. Why should I be?' countered Lee as coolly as she could, although inwardly she felt a cringe of distaste from the idea that her marriage to Max was a subject for gossip.

'Can't you guess?' demanded Sophy sharply. She was about sixty, and her iron grey hair was meticulously groomed in waves which swept back from her forehead. Her nose was long and curved downwards at the end, giving her a predatory look. 'Max Van Breedan has been one of our most eligible bachelors for some time, and now he's got married without any formal announcement, without inviting any of us to the wedding! There must have been a reason for all the rush and the privacy,' she went on. The small blue eyes narrowed and roved over Lee's slim taut figure as if searching for the reason for the rushed marriage, and realising with a jolt of distaste that the woman was implying that she was expecting Max's child, Lee felt anger mount slowly within her. She sat down on the chair next to Aunt Bertha, so that her figure was hidden from that predatory stare.

'I suppose it did seem a little unconventional,' Aunt Bertha put in suavely. 'But you know Max, Sophy. When he wants something he won't let anything stand in his way until he has got it. We had to consider Vincent, you know. He's been very ill these last two months, so Max thought that everything should be done quietly, with the minimum of fuss and publicity.'

'Humph! I still think it's strange that no one had ever seen this young woman in Max's company until two days before the wedding,' muttered Sophy, her bright gaze still

100

on Lee, watching for reactions.

'We met in England,' said Lee stiffly, wishing she could run away and hide as Juliana was doing.

'Then why didn't you marry there? It's usual to get married at the woman's place of abode there, isn't it?' asked Sophy sharply.

'Such a shame that they couldn't really,' Bertha said calmly. 'Max had to rush back here because Bruno was killed. So Lee flew out here when she was able to. I think it was very romantic to fly so far and be married on arrival.'

Sophy gave her a rather exasperated glance.

'You would,' she said dryly. 'You'd believe anything that devious devil told you too, Bertha. I guess it was a bit of a disappointment to your family over in England when you couldn't be married there,' she added, turning to Lee.

'I haven't any family,' replied Lee coolly.

'How convenient,' murmured Sophy. '*Ja*, very convenient under the circumstances.' And Lee felt apprehension trickle through her. This woman had guessed that Max had made a marriage of convenience.

'Beatrix is very upset,' Sophy announced with typical abruptness.

'Naturally. Eric's death was so sudden,' agreed Bertha consolingly.

'I wasn't referring to that,' said Sophy caustically. 'She's got over that now, as well as the fact that he didn't leave her a guilder, or perhaps I should say a dollar. In fact he died in debt.'

'Then perhaps it's the takeover.' Bertha was still serene as she turned to Lee. 'I should explain. Volney's Gifts Ltd. is the business Hans Volney left to Sophy when he died. Max had been trying to negotiate a takeover of the business to make it a branch of the Trading Company.'

'We don't go in for the expensive type of gift, and we're not jewellers,' Sophy took up the explanation. 'Our appeal

101

has always been to the tourist who has less money in his pocket, to the Venezuelans who like to buy gadgets made in the States. No, it isn't the takeover which is upsetting Beatrix, although I know she would prefer a partnership, as she sees in our shops a way of earning her living. It's the news of Max's marriage which has upset her. You know very well, Bertha, that at one time it was Hans' and my dearest wish that they should marry, and I've been hoping since Beatrix became a widow that the wish would come true at last.'

'Now who's romancing?' accused Bertha lightly, winking one bright eye at Lee. 'Take the guitar, Lee, and go in to see Vincent. He's been asking for you.'

Lee stood up obediently, glad to have an excuse to leave a conversation which was beginning to embarrass her.

'I'm pleased to have met you, Mrs Volney,' she said politely.

'You're being removed,' accused the woman harshly, 'you're being sent on your way before I say anything which might upset you. Your husband and my daughter were inseparable for years. Then Max was removed—sent to Europe by his father—and while he was away my girl was tempted into marriage by a man much older than herself. By the time Max returned she was settled in the States. Now you know why he's remained a bachelor for so long.'

'Sophy, that's enough!' Bertha's voice was quiet but imperious.

'No, it isn't. You,' here Sophy pointed at Lee, 'you might have Max's name, but you don't have his love. Beatrix has that and always will have it.'

'I must go now to see my father-in-law,' said Lee steadily, and turned towards the house.

'Vincent dotes on her already,' she heard Bertha saying. 'More tea, Sophy?'

As Lee moved through the old house on her way to

Vincent's room, one question surged to the fore. Was it true? Had Max remained a bachelor for so long because he had once been in love with Beatrix, who had married another man? Max in love! Her nerves tingled alarmingly at the thought. It was difficult to imagine the man of ice who was her husband being so deeply in love with a woman that he had not been able to marry anyone else. Until now! Her thoughts swirled like a whirlpool and she paused for a moment, hand on the doorknob, until they had steadied.

When she entered Vincent's room she found him sitting in his wheelchair close to the wide-open window which overlooked the gallery. Placed as he was, she realised he must have overheard everything Sophy Volney had been saying.

His tired grey eyes lit up when he saw her.

'I was hoping you would come. Sit here,' he said.

She sat on a cushioned stool close to him.

'You deserve to hear ill of yourself,' she rebuked him with a smile as she pointed to the open window.

'I have, I have,' he said, chuckling gleefully, then sobering, he added, 'Max tells me he is taking you to Aruba tomorrow to meet Irene and to stay at a hotel for a few days. That is understandable. You are young and like to dance and play. You've been very patient staying here for the last two weeks to please me—I hope you haven't found it dull?'

'No, it's been very pleasant,' she replied truthfully.

'You're a good girl, Leonora.' Ever since she had told him how she had come by her name he had used it in full. 'And because you are, I'm going to give you some advice, if you'll listen.'

'I'll listen.'

'While you've been here it has been easy for you, you've been protected to a certain extent by Bertha and myself. In Aruba you'll be on your own, so you must be careful. Your relationship with Max has been built quickly and because

103

of that it is precarious. One little push, and over it goes to tumble in ruins. It's vulnerable to all sorts of pressures because you don't know each other very well, and that isn't surprising since you met for the first time two weeks ago.'

Lee had been plucking idly at the strings of the guitar. Now she raised her head and looked at him. His grey eyes were still twinkling, but there was an expression of anxiety behind the twinkle.

'How did you guess?' she asked slowly.

'I didn't guess. I asked Max the day he brought you here. You see, I was very worried after I'd told him that I wanted him to get married, because he was angry.'

'Why?'

'He didn't like the threat I used to bring him into line. He flung out of here in a rage, swearing he'd marry the first single girl he laid eyes on, so I was worried, very worried, thinking that perhaps for once I had miscalculated. Max rarely gets angry, but when he does he acts without thinking. He could have married anyone in that frame of mind, so I had to ask him where he found you. I thought at first he was going to lie to me, but he must have sensed my anxiety and told me the truth. Today I decided I must tell you that I know why you came to Curaçao and what you hoped for; to tell you that I'm glad you didn't find Adrian Hartog and that Max had the good sense to persuade you to marry him.'

'I didn't have much alternative,' she murmured, 'except deportation.'

Vincent nodded.

'I know, but you made a choice which has made me very happy, and I thank you for it.'

'Would you mind telling me what threat you used?' she asked tentatively.

'I told him I'd cut him out of my will if he didn't marry and settle down before his next birthday.' He chuckled

104

again. 'He ran it very close, getting married as he did, on his birthday.'

'He told me he was being blackmailed by a very stubborn man,' she said with a smile. 'But would you have carried out such a threat if he hadn't got married?'

He gave her a long level look, then smiled and reached out to pat her hand.

'No, I wouldn't, although it has never been my custom to threaten idly, and Max knows that. But I was worried about him. I was afraid this last child of Carlotta's and of mine was going to go through life not knowing what it is to love and to be loved. You could say I felt guilty because I had, in my extreme grief when Carlotta died, ignored him and neglected him. The threat was the only way I could find to deal with him on the subject of marriage. I knew there were women in his life, but none of them were suitable to be his wife. I had to do something about it, and I chose the only weapon I had.'

He sighed and leaned back in his chair to close his eyes. Lee waited.

'The threat worked. He's married to as nice a young woman I could wish for. You're a little inexperienced for such a tough character as my son, but you've got spirit and you're as sound as a good English apple at heart. Or as sound as a good Dutch one, for that matter,' he added with a thin chuckle. 'Now play *The Bluebird* to me, once more.'

'Before I do, could you tell me something else, please? Was Mrs Volney telling the truth when she said you sent Max to Europe to remove him from her daughter?'

'Mmm. I heard her say that,' he replied, the thin skin of his forehead pleating in a frown. 'Yes, I arranged for Max to go and work with my cousin Walter, who has a similar business to ours in Holland. I wanted Max to learn the business from a connoisseur. I couldn't teach him myself, he and I are too alike for that to work, so I sent him to Walter.

He was friendly with Beatrix at the time, but he didn't object to going; not because he wanted to work for Walter, but because he wanted to take part in some sailing championship which was being held that year in Holland. He went, won the championship and stayed with Walter for three years.'

'When did he come back here?' Lee queried.

'When I became ill. Bruno couldn't manage alone. He needed a prop, so Max came back to help him.' Vincent sighed again. 'Now play *The Bluebird*, my dear.'

She could see he was very tired, so she pushed all disturbing thoughts and questions to the back of her mind and played and sang to him. The sun went down. The room was filled briefly with rosy light which was replaced by deep blue shadows that deepened to velvety black gloom.

Ending with a sweet Cuban lullaby, Lee rose to her feet and switched on a bedside lamp. By its light she could see that Vincent was asleep, his head drifting sideways. She would have to call Josh, his nurse. She turned towards the door and quivered with shock, for Max was standing there. Absorbed in making music, she had not heard him enter, and now she wondered how long he had been there, watching and listening.

'He was very tired,' she whispered, almost apologetically because she had sung Vincent to sleep.

'That lullaby sung the way you sing it would bring sleep to the most anxious and weary of people,' he replied quietly, and again she felt that flush of pleasure which she had experienced on the beach in the morning when he had praised her.

'I thought perhaps you wanted to talk to him,' she said.

'I did, but it's better for him to sleep.'

He opened the door and they both went out into the passage, where a single lamp glowed yellow. Looking at Max, Lee saw he was frowning and that there was a hint of strain about the controlled mouth.

'Your father told me of the threat he used to get you to marry before your birthday,' she said.

Surprise peaked his eyebrows. Humour chased the coldness from his eyes and softened the line of his mouth.

'So now you know I married you for money,' he scoffed softly. 'His money.'

'Oh!' She was disconcerted. She had not seen it in that light before. His mocking admission had the effect of cooling down the flush of pleasure rapidly. 'But you said it was to make him happy.'

'And that was true, because he wouldn't have been happy if he had had to leave the control of the business to someone else just because I refused to comply with his wishes. So I complied and married the first single woman I came across who fitted in with his requirements. It seems to have worked out satisfactorily. He's happy.'

A feeling of disappointment was fast mushrooming within her, blanketing every other feeling with its grey desolation. But why should she feel disappointed? What had she expected him to say? That he had married her for some other reason?

'And his will?' She forced the question through stiff lips.

'Signed and sealed—yesterday.' He sounded complacent. And why not? His quick businesslike marriage had paid off. Another success could be chalked up, brought about by his ability to seize an opportunity when it offered and turn it to his advantage.

Outrage blazed up suddenly, burning off the grey smoke of disappointment. Lee had a feeling that she had been used by him, like a pawn in a game he was playing, and like the pawn, when her use was over, she would be discarded.

'You deceived me!' she accused him.

His reaction was a sharp turning of his head, a glinting in his eyes. He did not like her accusation, that was obvious.

'I did? In what way?'

'You didn't tell me anything about money or a will,' she faltered, slightly put off by his cool surprise. 'You didn't tell me what threat he was using. I suppose you guessed I'd have refused to marry you if I'd known it was for your own personal gain.'

He folded his arms across his chest and leaned against the wall, studying her with a sharp penetrating gaze.

'I didn't have to guess. I *knew* you'd throw up your hands in horror at the thought of marrying me in cold blood just to help me make sure of my inheritance, so I left out that part. You can call it deception, if you like, I call it good sense. I was in a difficult position. If I refused to bow to Vincent's demands I stood to lose everything I've ever worked for—the control of the company. Put yourself in my position, ask yourself what you would have done. My common sense recommended me to get married—I had two days left to find a suitable wife when you were dropped by some beneficent god into Willemstad two weeks ago. I'd have been very foolish if I'd frightened you away with talk of wills and money.'

He paused and frowned. Uncertainty darkened his eyes for a moment, then was gone, leaving them as clear and as cold as ice-water.

'Now that I've told you everything, what do you intend to do?' he asked.

What could she do? Leave? Where could she go? She didn't have enough money to buy a ticket on a plane bound for Europe, and she couldn't stay on the island unless she could convince the authorities she had enough money to support herself. She was still dependent on this man's goodwill and protection whether she wanted to be or not.

'The rest still stands, you know,' he said, persuasion

softening his voice. 'Vincent is happy and he's still alive, so I still need a wife he'll accept. If you like him as much as I believe you do, you won't run out on me as Bruno's wife did on him. To desert me now—and that's how it would look—just because you've discovered something about me you don't like would do irreparable damage to my father's feelings and would defeat the main object I had for marrying you, to make him happy.'

'And it would make him change the will?' Lee challenged rather weakly, for a strange fear was sweeping over her, a fear of that devilish insight of his into the way her mind worked. He knew which words and arguments would sway her. He knew she would not desert him while Vincent was alive. Her own pride and integrity, her sense of loyalty would not let her.

'Perhaps.' His answer was noncommittal. His face was expressionless.

'Well, you needn't worry, I won't desert you,' she said in a low furious voice. 'But you can be sure it won't be because I have any feelings concerning you. It'll be because you're right as usual, I couldn't hurt your father for anything. I'll stay with you until he dies.'

For the second time that day an outburst of hers created an atmosphere of agonising, twanging tension. Standing straight and still, clutching Carlotta Van Breedan's beautiful guitar against her, Lee waited for Max to retaliate.

Maybe now he'll get into a rage, she found herself hoping, half fearfully, half excitedly. Maybe now he'll act without thinking.

Almost as if he had guessed what had passed through her mind and was determined not to do as she expected, he dropped his gaze, and she was baffled as always by the taut darkness of his face, unlit by the light eyes. A faint smile lifted his long upper lip.

'Thank you. That's all I needed to know. Aunt Bertha

has suggested we stay for dinner tonight since we're going away in the morning, so I'll see you later. I'll go and fetch Josh now to attend to my father,' he said coolly.

He went away down the passage, leaving her with the strangest feeling that he had won yet another skirmish when victory, by rights, should have been hers.

CHAPTER FIVE

LEE did her best to be cool and self-contained during dinner, to ignore Max in the way he often ignored her, reminding herself that in a business arrangement such as theirs she should keep her emotions under control at all times.

She succeeded fairly well, but at a cost to herself. Being of a naturally warm and friendly disposition she had never been able to keep up a cold war with anyone for long; bottling up feelings tended to be dangerous for one of her temperament. If she didn't let off steam occasionally, she was likely to explode in all directions.

So by the time she went to bed she was feeling exhausted with the effort of being cool and controlled, and was glad to be alone in the moonlit quiet of her room to lie down, hoping to relax quickly and fall asleep.

But inevitably, because she had given way to her emotions during the day, everything that had happened between herself and Max came back into her mind to torment her. Ever since she had married him she had been making an effort to behave as he had suggested she should behave, showing only affection in public then trying to turn it off, as one turns off a tap or switches off a light, when they were alone. The resulting strain on her had caused her to explode today, she was sure; on the beach, at lunch-time and then later outside his father's room. Three times she had shown that everything he did or said affected her far more than it should.

Why? The question stood out in the blackness of her mind written in big white letters. Why? Why?

Turning restlessly on the bed, she tried to blot it out, tried to think of something else more soothing, but all that would come were images of Max.

Max concerned, because he had thought she had hurt herself when sailing. Max showing humour and patience, offering to ease the discomfort she felt when alone with him by suggesting a change of scene. Max playing the guitar skilfully, surprising her. Max with a gentleness which had unnerved her, showing he understood her difficulties in adjusting to being married. Yes, he had been almost tender in his attempt to sympathise with her, and if Juliana hadn't come just then ...

Lee's breath caught in her throat. Once again she turned restlessly, trying to blot that tender moment that had happened in the soporific silence of the afternoon from her memory. Deliberately she thought of Max's reaction to her accusation that he had deceived her by not telling her everything about Vincent's threat. Again he had been cool, but he had been honest too, and in return she had behaved like a shrew, flaring out at him again.

She wriggled miserably. Max might be cool and unemotional, brisk and businesslike, always having a good thought-out reason for everything he did, but he had never been unkind—and in the light of his mature, considerate behaviour her own seemed like that of a spoilt, bad-tempered child.

Somehow she must try and make more effort to understand him as obviously he was making effort to understand her. She could start by trying to understand how he had felt when faced with Vincent's threat.

He had been angry. That proved that he wasn't always as cool and emotional as he appeared to be. He had flung out of the house swearing to marry the first girl he met. But his rage had cooled down: he had considered the alternative and had seen that if he did not do what Vincent asked him to do he would be bypassed and rejected as his father had always bypassed and rejected him. And he had been determined not to let that happen again.

Placed in the same circumstances, would she have behaved any differently herself? Wouldn't she have protected her own interests? As sleep weighted heavily on her eyelids at last, Lee felt forgiveness sweeping over her in a lovely warm sensation, liberating her feelings towards Max. He had not told her about his father's will because it was none of her business, and as he had said the rest still stood. Their marriage had made an old man happy.

Next morning she awoke clear-eyed and in good spirits, the cold war forgotten. At breakfast she chattered away to Max as if nothing had happened the previous evening. Once or twice she caught him looking at her in an amused way, but excited by the forthcoming trip—especially when he told her that they would be flying to Aruba in the Company's four-seater plane which he would pilot himself —she refused to let anything dampen her spirits.

Right up to the time of their departure for the airport she hoped she would see Juliana again, and had even gone to the girl's room hoping to find her there. The possibility of leaving without having talked to the girl worried her a little, so that she mentioned it to Aunt Bertha as they kissed goodbye.

'She has the sulks for some reason,' said the kind, serene old lady. 'I expect she'll be over them by the time you see her again. I've always found it best to leave her alone when she behaves that way. Now off you go, my dear, and enjoy yourself, and give my love to Irene, Claus and young Pieter.'

The little blue car had gone some way along the winding tamarind-shaded driveway before Max asked abruptly,

'Why is Julie sulking?'

'It's difficult to say. When we were talking yesterday

113

after her lesson she said that someone once told her that you wished she'd been killed with her father, and that she's in your way and a nuisance to you. When I tried to find out more, she ran away.'

She watched his face for a change of expression. His sunglasses made it difficult for her to read it, but she noticed his jaw muscles tighten as his mouth curved sardonically.

'If she believes that, it's no wonder she avoids me as if I have some infectious disease,' he murmured with a touch of bitterness.

'Is she in your way?'

'I suppose you believe she could be now that you know to what lengths I've been prepared to go to preserve my inheritance,' he accused, still bitter, and she answered quickly.

'No, no, I don't believe that! It wasn't a very nice thing for anyone to say about you, but I don't think Julie would have said it if she hadn't heard it from someone else. She listens a lot to family gossip and picks up some very strange ideas. I thought perhaps she might have heard Aunt Bertha and your sister say something which she's got twisted. They discuss you a lot, she says.'

'Do they?' He seemed amused. 'And which of my many activities do they find worthy of discussion?'

'From what Julie tells me, I gather they've often wondered which of your many girl-friends you might marry,' she replied lightly, daring to tease him a little. Glancing sideways, she was relieved to see he had taken her teasing in good part and was smiling.

'Smoke-screen,' he said laconically.

'What do you mean?' Lee questioned blankly.

'The many girl-friends have provided a smoke-screen so that no one could guess where my real interests might lie, that's all.'

She was silent. Did his reply mean that his interest was, and had been for years, Beatrix Deering, who had married someone else but was now a widow?

'I don't think Aunt Bertha or Irene would say that Julie is in my way,' he went on thoughtfully. 'They know that Bruno left her well provided for, and made me her guardian to look after her finances until she's old enough to look after them herself. He couldn't leave her any share in the business because he had no share, no more than I have. My father still has full control and will only leave it to a male heir. Possibly if Bruno had survived he would have split the business between us.'

'But why couldn't any of it be left to a woman, to your sister or to Julie?'

'Haven't you noticed that Vincent is a little old-fashioned and traditional in his thinking? He believes a woman's place is in the home and that her job is to be a source of comfort and joy to her husband, as my mother was to him.'

'But it isn't fair! Your sister or Julie could have inherited the Van Breedan business acumen just as much as you have,' she objected hotly. 'Why should they be by-passed?'

'All right, spitfire,' he scoffed, 'keep cool. I agree with you. Women can be as good at business management as men can be, as my sister has proved by opening her own business. But there's nothing we can do about it in our family until Vincent dies. How did Julie come to tell you that she believed herself to be in my way?'

'I asked her to come and live with us in Willemstad.' Max gave her a quick sideways glance of surprise and she added hurriedly: 'Well, you did say I was to try and help her, and I think she should go back to school. And to do that she has to live in Willemstad. I know I should have discussed it with you first, but the idea came to me suddenly when she said she liked being with me and having

115

me to talk to. It seemed a good idea, and . . .'

'It is,' he interrupted her curtly, 'so you can stop defending it. I'm surprised because you feel you can commit yourself to so much so soon. But then I'd forgotten how reckless you can be.'

Lee wasn't quite sure how to take such a remark and was silent for a while, thinking it over. But it didn't make much sense to her, so she said with a sigh:

'I don't seem to have helped at all. I'm right back at square one with her. It'll be much harder to win her confidence now—I was in too much of a rush, as usual.'

To her surprise he took a hand off the steering wheel and patted hers consolingly where they lay on her lap.

'Don't worry about it. Perhaps it's as well we're going away for a few days. She'll have time to miss you. By the time we return from Aruba we might know what she meant when she said she was in my way. Irene might know; her boutique is the first place I'm going to take you when we reach Orenjestad. You need clothes.'

The flat statement left Lee in no doubt as to what he thought of her small wardrobe, but her pride was up in arms at once.

'I have some, thank you.'

'I know, but not the right sort. Where we're going to stay people are going to stare at you because you're my wife and not because you're pretty. They're going to look at everything you wear and assess how much it cost me to put it on your back, so I can't have you looking shabby.'

'Oh, how horrible!' she exclaimed, thoroughly revolted at the idea of being looked over in such a way. 'I shall feel even more like a piece of merchandise you've picked up on your travels.'

'But you are, *lieveling*, you are,' he jeered softly. 'You're my bargain bride. Had you forgotten?'

Lieveling. Dutch for darling. Lee's fingers curled under,

116

making her hands into fists as she controlled a longing to reject the endearment. His casual use of it showed a change of attitude on his part, as if he were really regarding her as a possession.

Confused, she looked out at the passing scene. They were on the road going south-east across the island to the airport. Giant cacti cast fantastic shadows on the sun-baked earth. The road wound through a village and as the car slowed down she realised how familiar the sun-washed, red-roofed houses had become to her. Thick-walled, slit-windowed for coolness within, solid and foursquare like the Dutchmen who had colonised the island. A few palms lent a touch of exoticism to the scene and the sound of a *tambu*, a jungle drum beating out African rhythms, a legacy of the time of slavery, hinted at a sensuality quite at variance with the cool solid buildings.

Lee's glance drifted back to Max. Not for the first time she thought how his black hair and swarthy complexion gave his blunt-featured face a certain exoticism, how that enigmatic mouth of his hinted at a sensuality which was not apparent in his behaviour.

But he should not call her *lieveling*. He wasn't in love with her and she wasn't his darling. He had married her for convenience so that a will would be made in his favour. Now that will was signed and sealed and would remain like that as long as she stayed married to him until Vincent Van Breedan died.

But what would happen when the old man had passed away? Would Max Van Breedan want his bargain bride any more? Wouldn't he want to be free of the shackles which bound him to her? Those shackles would be easy to snap. Annulment of a marriage such as theirs would be easy and painless.

The direction of her thoughts kept her silent for the rest of the drive and Max was, as usual, uncommunicative. At

117

the airport the big jet-liners glittered in the sunlight and the noise of their engines was deafening. The little blue and white twin-engined four-seater aeroplane was ready for them. The propeller was swung, the engines leapt into life. The brakes were released, and having received clearance from the control tower by radio, Max taxied it to the end of a runway, made sure no other plane was about to land and opened the throttle smoothly.

As speed increased the runway at each side became blurred. The engine noise was lost in the sound of air rushing past the plane. For a few seconds Lee was conscious of a barrage of sensations as the nose of the plane lifted and it was airborne.

Watching Max as he checked the altimeter and replied to the control tower, Lee wondered if there was anything he couldn't do. Successful businessman, champion dinghy sailor, accomplished guitar-player and now competent aviator, he seemed capable of anything, and his cool competence cut her off from him so that she saw him as someone remote and mysterious, almost godlike.

'Don't look so worried!' he shouted at her above the roar of the engine. 'You're quite safe.'

'I'm not worried, just amazed.'

'Because I can fly this thing?'

'Yes. Is there anything you can't do?'

'Not much when I set my mind to it,' he answered with a tantalising grin. 'But lots of people can fly planes. There's nothing to it. Like to try?'

'Now?' she squeaked.

'Yes.'

She glanced out of the window. Below, the coastline was passing beneath them, a rim of white sand edged by creamy foam. Pale green water covered the dark shapes of rocks. A catamaran with a black and white striped sail ran before the wind looking for all the world like a butterfly. Then it was

118

gone and the sea was beneath them, like an expanse of ruched blue satin embroidered with white flecks where the crests of waves broke.

Lee looked in front of her. There was a panel of instruments just like the panel in front of Max. There was also a white handle such as the one he was holding, which was presumably the control. If she made a mistake he could correct it, because the plane had dual controls. It would be like driving a car. Why shouldn't she try?

'What do I do?' she shouted at him, and saw him grin again.

'Good for you!' he replied. 'We're now on course and at the right altitude. All you have to do is keep the wings level. Look at the wing tips now and see where they are in relation to the horizon. You have also to watch the nose. The altimeter will tell you if you're losing height or gaining it.'

When she first took over the nose of the plane dipped downwards in a terrifying way, but by following Max's instructions she soon had it up again. Keeping the plane level was not easy, and anyone watching from below must have wondered why the plane was waggling its wings so much.

At last she began to get the feel of the machine, to sense when it was level. It zoomed on, not dancing over the sea as the sailing dinghy had done, but dancing through the air, and joy surged up in Lee; joy which had to be shared with the person who had made it possible. She turned to look at Max, found him watching her, and smiled at him. He smiled back, and at once, like the hunter in the song she had sung so often, she was caught in the web of love.

The plane's nose dipped alarmingly. Its starboard wing tilted up, pointing to the sky.

'You have to concentrate,' shouted Max mockingly as she glanced with alarm at the instruments and tried to correct the level of the plane. 'No time for romancing up here.'

His last jeer alarmed Lee more than the side-slipping of the plane had done. Romancing! Was that really what she had been doing, reading more into that intimate moment of shared joy than had been in it? If that were the case she must get down to earth quickly. The footless halls and the delirious burning blue of the sky were not for her.

Once she had levelled the plane and had flown it for about half an hour, Max took over the controls again. The dark shape which was Aruba had come closer, showing a ridge of small hills like a spine. Soon they were flying in over another rim of sand, edged by pale green sea, climbing up over the low hills and seeing the shadow of the plane, like that of a giant moth, darkening the amber-coloured land. The sea appeared again like a sheet of beaten silver under the sun's rays. Another coastline wound its way northwards; they followed its shining rim until buildings appeared, rectangles and squares of colour, the town of Orenjestad.

Max received permission to land from the control tower, and soon the little plane was taxiing along the runway towards the airport buildings.

As they walked away from the plane Max said casually,

'One day I'll show you how to take off and land, if you would like that.'

Joy surged up uncontrollably. Without thinking Lee turned to him, saw the glint of mockery in his eyes and looked away again, chewing on her lips uncertainly. She did not want to be accused of romancing again.

'Thank you, I'd like that,' she said woodenly.

They went to the town by taxi and within a few minutes Lee was stepping through a door into the wide square hallway of an old house similar to the Van Breedan town house in Willemstad. A young woman came through an archway

120

that opened into a room to the right. Max spoke to her in Dutch, and she smiled and went back into the room. In a few seconds another woman appeared. She was tall, her curly hair was raven black, her complexion was tawny gold and her wide eyes were a dark velvety brown. She was almost the exact replica of the picture of Carlotta Van Breedan which was in Vincent's room.

'Max!' she exclaimed, and without hesitation went up to him and kissed him affectionately. Then she noticed Lee. Her eyes went wide and she put a slender hand to her mouth.

'*Por dios, amigo,*' she said in a comical whisper, 'what have you done this time? She can't be your new wife!'

'What do you mean by "new"?' countered Max. 'I've never had a wife before. Lee, meet my sister Irene. You two should have much in common. Neither of you think before you speak,' he added acidly.

'Forgive me, I did not mean to be rude,' said Irene, taking Lee's hand in both of hers. 'But you are so young, too young for this cynic who is my brother.'

'Lee needs clothes,' said Max curtly. 'Everything from the skin out.'

'Oh, I don't!' began Lee, turning on him fierily.

'Hush,' admonished Irene softly, her eyes twinkling. 'He's right. Unfortunately for the rest of us he always is. You cannot go to stay at the hotel as his wife unless you have the best.' Her eyes narrowed as she surveyed Lee. 'I have a dream of an evening gown for you. Sea-green, cut on Grecian lines. With you hair swept up so ...' Here Irene stepped forward and with both hands swept Lee's hair on top of her head. 'You will look like the goddess of the sea herself.'

'Since I'll be paying,' said Max matter-of-factly, 'I'll want to have final say on everything, so there'll be no doing this behind closed doors.'

'But no, *señor*, of course not,' said Irene mockingly, 'we shall go upstairs to the private showing rooms. This way.'

'Do you even want to see the underwear?' asked Lee, turning to Max.

'Maybe I'll pass that up,' he replied with a taunting grin, taking her arm and urging her towards the stairs. 'Unless the price seems sky-high. Then I'll want to see it ... on you.'

Almost two hours later Lee slumped exhausted into a chair in the changing room. In spite of the air-conditioning she felt like a limp rag, and perspiration was springing out of her pores. Trying on clothes, parading before Max as he lounged on a settee covered in gold brocade in the beautifully furnished showing room, had been exhausting both physically and mentally. Wreathed in cigar smoke, he had studied each item of clothing, made comments to his sister and then had decided either for or against.

Sometimes, aggravated because he had disliked some dress which she liked, she had objected to his veto and there had been a battle of words, hers hot and choked, his crisp and icy. She had given in only when she had realised that nothing she said would make him change his mind; or when Irene intervened, agreeing with Max and pointing out quietly how a certain style made her look either too old or too childish.

All the time she was showing the clothes she was aware of the easy, chaffing conversation which went on between sister and brother. In front of her they spoke English and talked only about things she would know about: Vincent's health, Juliana's slow recovery; Irene's husband Claus, who worked for the big oil company which had refineries on the island, and her impish son Pieter. From the conversation she learned that Irene, wanting to be in business but banned from the trading company by her father's refusal to let the women of his family work in it, had set up her boutique with the assistance of Max. It was thriving to such an extent that she was hoping to open another one in Willemstad.

But when she was alone in the changing room she heard them talking in Spanish, the language in which Irene was obviously more at ease, it having been her mother's tongue. Irene's voice, though low, expressed anxiety, and Max sounded as if he were reassuring her about something. Lee wondered if it was his recent rushed marriage that was under discussion.

Now the clothes were being packed and Max was writing out a cheque for the amount which they had cost. Lee had no doubts that it was a large amount of money, enough to pay her fare back to England, even though Max had not been above haggling with his sister over the price of some of the more exclusive gowns.

The curtain which closed the changing room off from the other room was swept aside. Irene came in, carrying a suit made from pale pink tussore silk.

'You are to wear this for going to the hotel,' she said. Her quick brown eyes noted the pallor of Lee's face, the way she was slumped in the chair, and her face softened. 'I know that was tough on you,' she sympathised, 'but believe me, you'll be glad in the next few days that Max had the sense to bring you to me to dress you. Most of the people staying at the hotel will be tourists, it is true, but there will be some who will know Max—international jet-setters, social lights, government bureaucrats—who come here to relax for a while and who shop at the Van Breedan stores. They will be interested in you, so you must look your best for him at all times. With your youth, your colouring and natural prettiness it will not be difficult. You're going to look stunning in some of those gowns he has chosen, and he knows it. He has a very good eye for colour, you know, and excellent taste in design. In some respects he is a greater connoisseur than my father.'

Something burst in Lee.

'But I don't want and never have wanted to look stunning,' she objected, giving expression to the rebellion which was exploding inside her against a way of life she had never wanted to follow, that of the wife kept as a showpiece to enhance her husband's position and worth. 'I want to be myself! I want to be loved for myself, not for what I'm wearing or how I look or because I'm married to Max Van Breedan!'

Irene's dark eyes showed a certain coolness as she slipped the skirt of the suit off its hanger and handed it to Lee.

'Don't we all want to be loved for what we are?' she murmured. 'But how often does that happen? If you can find someone to love you for what you are and not for how you look or what you can offer or give, you'll be very lucky. And while we are on the subject I could ask you why you love Max. Is it for what he is? Or is it for his wealth and position? Or possibly it's for what he has been able to do for you?'

Lee was suddenly busy with the zip of the skirt which she had slipped on, taking longer to do it up than necessary because she could not face Irene and give an honest answer.

'You see,' accused Irene softly, 'you cannot answer. It is because you do not love him at all, for any reason.'

The accusation stung. It implied that she was a hypocrite, made her realise how she must appear to this graceful woman who obviously had a great fondness for Max. Lee's head went up sharply in reaction, to defend herself against the implication.

'That isn't true!' she blurted. 'I do love him ...' She stopped short, amazed at her own impulsive confession of love as she saw Irene's eyes narrow sceptically, and she added belatedly, 'A little.'

Irene's mouth took on a sardonic curve, giving her a fleeting resemblance to Max.

'A little,' she mocked. 'I think any woman could love a little a man who provided her with all these clothes, a roof over her head and food to eat, as well as the protection of his good name. Yes, gratitude can often be mistaken for love, be a substitute for it.'

Lee gulped hard to quell the hot tears which had sprung into her eyes.

'Max must have told you why he married me,' she said in a low shaken voice.

'*Si*, I know why he has married you. I know also that you came out to Curaçao hoping to marry another man.' Irene paused in the doorway before lifting the velvet curtain. 'The pity of it all is,' she added in cool tones, 'if Max could have waited a while, he would not have had to marry a stranger. He could have married someone he has known for years and who loves him.'

The curtain was raised, then fell into place with a swish and a ripple of golden light as Irene left the small room. Biting her lower lip, Lee blinked back more tears. Her heart was hammering, filling her ears with its beat. With a few succinct words Irene had conveyed her distaste for Max's marriage of convenience and had made it very clear that she had no use for a woman who had agreed to marry him without loving him.

With fingers that shook, she fastened the front of the short jacket which went with the pleated skirt, slipping the big pearl buttons through the hand-sewn buttonholes. She combed her hair, applied some pale lipstick, and stepped back from the mirror to take a last look at herself. The pale pink of the suit was certainly flattering. It set off the creaminess of her complexion and at the same time sparked off fresh glints of copper in her hair. She looked slim, cool and, surprisingly, a little remote because her golden-brown eyes, which tilted upwards slightly at the corners, had a withdrawn expression as her thoughts were busy with the conversation that had just taken place between herself and Irene.

She had no doubt that the someone Max had known for years was Beatrix Deering, who was now back in Curaçao, a widow and free to marry Max. But Beatrix had returned too late, because Max was married to Lee, and would have to stay married to her until his father died.

And what of her own blurted confession that she loved Max—a little? It had been made in self-defence because she had not liked Irene's insinuation that she was just a free-loader, a scrounger getting as much out of Max as she could in return for appearing as his wife.

'The taxi has come to take you to the hotel.' Irene was back, standing in front of the curtain of golden velvet, an excellent background for her dark colouring. 'Yes, you look well in that suit, but a little sad. You must smile, be gay, show you are happy to be married. Otherwise people will guess the truth, and we can't have that happening, can we? And before you go, may I give you another word of advice? We Van Breedans are very conventional, especially in our public behaviour. We do not like scandal. My eldest brother's wife did not understand this. Like you, she had a more unconventional attitude to life; she thought she could do as she liked without consideration for how her actions might appear to outsiders. When reminded that she was behaving without due consideration for Bruno, she defended her actions by saying she was a person in her own right and had to *do her own thing*.'

Irene paused. The twinkle came back into her eyes and she bent and kissed Lee lightly on the cheek. ' "A little," ' she murmured. 'You know, given the right warmth and

126

nourishment a little could grow into a lot. Come now, Max is waiting.'

The taxi driver was garrulous, chattering away in Papiementu to Max. In her corner of the back seat Lee leaned back and looked out of the window at the sparkling streets; at the new hotel building, blocks of concrete and glass glittering in the brilliant sunlight, at the weirdly right-angled divi-divi trees and the cactus-like aloes.

The taxi swept off the road into a courtyard before one of the hotels. A uniformed door attendant opened the door for her to step out, and a bellboy was summoned to take care of the luggage and the clothes boxes from Irene's boutique. In a shining spacious rose and blue entrance hall, Lee was conscious of being greeted with deference as well as pleasure by the desk clerk. Lift doors swept open silently. With Max and the bellboy she was whisked upwards. The doors opened again and she went down a thickly carpeted corridor which was lined by discreet-looking doors.

A key was produced, a door unlocked, and Lee went first into a wide room, shaded by venetian blinds against the strong sun. It was a room like a sea-cave, full of bluish-green light reflected off its sea-green walls and ultramarine carpet. It had a wide canopied bed covered in white drap-eries, lacy and delicate like sea-foam.

Doors were opened by the bellboy as he showed off the big bathroom, the little vanity-room and the second bed-room, smaller and decorated in orange and brown. Max's luggage was placed in that room; the communicating door was closed and at last Lee was alone.

In a silence which was broken only by the sound of the sea as it washed on the shore below the window, Lee eased off her white sling-back shoes. A knock on the outer door alerted her, and she went to open it. A smiling brown-skinned waitress was there with a tray on which there was lunch for one. It was placed on a small table and the waitress left. As she poured welcome tea for herself and ate the delicious sandwiches, Lee found herself being grateful to Max for having ordered the meal and for having the consideration to let her eat it alone.

Grateful. Gratitude. A substitute for love. Irene's words returned to mock her. If only she had not reacted to that accusation made by Max's sister! That impulsive confession of hers that she did love Max a little was boomeranging on her. It was making her stop and think, analyse her own motives in marrying Max.

Smile, be gay, show you are happy to be married, Irene had also advised her, *or people will guess the truth.* But what was the truth?

Slowly Lee stood up and began to take off the tussore suit, hanging it in the walk-in closet. The long mirror on the door of the closet showed the reflection of a slim young woman wearing a white underslip of sheer nylon, edged with fine lace at the hem and at the deep V of its bodice.

The door from the outer bedroom opened suddenly and she turned defensively, wishing she had unpacked and that her dressing gown had been available. She was a little surprised that Max had entered without knocking. At the bungalow he had never entered her room once.

He was obviously in the process of changing, possibly slipping off his clothing to lie down on the bed for a siesta just as she had intended to do. His white shirt was undone and pulled out of the waistband of his grey trousers, and as always when casually dressed he looked tough and physically formidable.

He was carrying a slim box covered with black velvet in one hand, and as he closed the door behind him she saw his light eyes glint as he noted the tray on the table. His glance lifted to her.

'I see you've had lunch. Good. You'll feel better now,' he said, advancing a little into the room. 'I'd like to show you something. Come over here.'

He sat down, to her dismay, on the side of the bed, casually, as if he had a right to, and opened the box. She could see something gleaming with subtle opulence on the satin lining of the box and curiosity pushed her forward to look.

She gasped when she saw the necklace of fine emeralds, each one set in a mesh of gold filigree. It was an exquisite piece of jewellery, delicate and tasteful in its design, in the tradition of the jewellery which had been sold by the Van Breedan company for years.

'I'd like you to wear it while we're here,' said Max in his most matter-of-fact way.

'I couldn't!' she gasped.

He gave her a sharp underbrowed glance.

'Why not? It will look perfect with that sea-green gown.'

'Oh, can't you understand?' she pleaded. 'I can't accept or wear your jewellery. You've given me enough, and I've nothing to give in return.'

This time his glance came up more slowly, lingering on the shape of her figure in the almost sheer underslip.

'I wouldn't be too sure about that,' he murmured with a humorous quirk to his mouth, and Lee stepped back defensively, feeling very vulnerable.

He lifted the necklace from the box which he tossed aside on to the bed.

'Sit down here, beside me,' he ordered. 'I'd like to see how it looks on you.'

'No. I've dressed up enough for your entertainment today. All those clothes,' her hand gestured towards the unpacked boxes, 'this.' She pointed to the glowing necklace in his hands. 'They make me feel cheap, like ... like ... a kept woman.'

His eyebrows peaked in surprise. Then he laughed, that wicked chuckle which made her want to laugh with him.

'Which you are, *lieveling*. All wives are, although most of them don't like to admit it. Come on, sit down and turn your back to me so that I can fasten them round your neck. Why not think of the jewels as the wedding present I neglected to give you when we got married?'

He sounded as coolly reasonable as ever, humouring her, obviously not believing in her protests, as if he was used to women refusing his gifts and then giving in to him and accepting them.

'I don't want it and I won't wear it,' she said stubbornly, 'and I can't understand why you want me to wear it.'

He looked down at the necklace in his hands, thinking out an answer to her question.

'In a way it's to prove to people who know me that you're really my wife,' he replied at last, still reasonable. 'Everyone who knows the name Van Breedan automatically associates it with good jewellery, and they will expect to see you wearing something like this.'

'I see. So it's proof of possession!' she said in a low, furious voice. 'I might have guessed.'

His eyes flashed like lightning as he looked up at her.

'If you want to put it that way, I suppose it is,' he said. 'Do you find it offensive to be regarded as a possession of mine?'

There was a dangerous edge to his voice, and Lee's hands went to her burning cheeks as she sought desperately in her mind for some diplomatic explanation to avoid irritating him further, but lack of experience in dealing with a man of his pride, plus her innate honesty and sheer youthfulness of outlook, defeated her. All she could say was:

'Yes, I do, because it isn't true. I'm not a possession of yours.'

A strange expression flickered in the grey eyes watching her; she was reminded of the flicker of a pale violet flame sometimes seen rising from smoky coal. Then the ex-

130

pression was hidden as he looked down at the necklace again.

'So that's your problem,' he murmured enigmatically. 'Perhaps the time has come when I should do something about it.'

Puzzled, she stood poised ready for flight should he move towards her, but when he moved it was to pick up the velvet box. Moving with a slow deliberation which calmed her fears, he placed the necklace on its bed of white satin. She stepped a little nearer to take a last look at the beautiful thing, then the box closed with a snap and was placed on the bedside table, and the hand which had placed it there grasped her lax one. One pull and he had her sitting beside him on the bed.

At once she tried to struggle to her feet, but as well as tightening his grip on her hand he grasped her other arm with his free hand, the fingers biting like steel into her soft flesh.

'Stay still,' he commanded.

The sun-shot, sea-cool dimness of the lovely room re-minded her of the previous afternoon when he had been gentle, almost tender, when he had told her he was on the same voyage of discovery as herself.

But there was nothing gentle about him now. There was a cruelty in the bite of his fingers which made her want to cry out. Fear combined with protest within her and would not be contained. Flinging her hair back behind her shoulders, she looked at him steadily.

'You're hurting me,' she accused.

'Too bad,' he drawled through taut lips. 'I suppose you think you never hurt anyone, that you can say what you like and get away with it.'

That shocked her. She stopped trying to twist free from his grasp and stared at him, her eyes wide with disbelief. Surely she hadn't hurt him! If she had she was glad, glad

131

she had made him feel pain, because if he could feel pain he could feel other emotions too. And yet she was also sorry, because hurting anyone always recoiled on her so that she suffered and ached to make amends. She wanted to do that now, but for the life of her she could not imagine how she had hurt him or why.

'I didn't intend to hurt you,' she mumbled.

His fingers relaxed their hold a little but still held her arm. He moved his thumb gently and caressingly against the soft skin on the inside of her arm, as if he were trying to stroke away the pain.

'Nor did I intend to hurt you,' he replied softly, 'but it's inevitable that we hurt one another in this situation. I'd like to explain why I want you to wear the necklace. That is if you're willing to listen.'

All defiance gone, Lee nodded, lowering her eyes. Being so close to him, feeling his vibrant warmth beating out to her, knowing she had hurt him, all were having an effect on her. She longed to reach out to slide a hand inside his shirt to feel the leap of his heart under the taut bronzed skin of his chest. She wanted to touch the strong column of his neck, let her fingers trail upwards over his face to tangle in the black curls of his hair. Above all she wanted to lie against him and feel his arms holding her closely, as he had held her that first day in Willemstad.

'When we were staying at the bungalow it wasn't necessary to show much proof of possession, as you call it, because we were with members of the family,' he said quietly. 'But here we'll be observed more closely and with a great deal of curiosity. It's known that I married in haste, and anything which is lacking in our relationship will be noticed and commented upon. Do you understand?'

She nodded, recalling Vincent's warning of the previous day. Only an hour or so ago Irene too had given her some advice. People would guess the truth if some sort of show

132

wasn't put on, and whatever happened no scandal must be attached to the good name of Van Breedan.

'If you won't wear that necklace it'll be assumed that either I don't care enough about you to give you any jewellery, or that you don't care enough for me to wear anything I give you,' he went on coolly and reasonably.

'But we ...' Lee began, to stop abruptly as fingers tightened cruelly on her arm again.

'I know,' he interrupted curtly, 'you're going to tell me that it's true we don't care for each other. And I'm telling you I'd prefer it if the truth could be kept between us and not broadcast to the gossip-mongers. That clear?'

No scandal. Behave with decorum. Never give any hint to outsiders that everything wasn't as it should be in their marriage. Again she nodded to show she understood.

'Today my sister noticed a lack in you, so I was forced to explain to her why I married you, which was something I had hoped to avoid having to do,' he continued.

He meant she had not been playing her part well enough, had not been keeping her side of the bargain.

'I'm sorry,' she said hurriedly. 'She told me I should smile more, show that I'm happy to be married to you, be gay—and I will, Max. I promise I will.'

'That isn't what she said to me. She said that anyone who knows me well will never believe you've been my wife for two whole weeks.'

'Oh, why wouldn't they?' she asked, feeling puzzled.

'Because you look untouched and unloved, she said. Could be she meant unpossessed,' he drawled suggestively; and releasing her arm, he put a knuckle under her chin and turned her face towards the window so that it was illuminated by a stray beam of sunlight shafting in through the slats of the blind. 'Looking at you closely I'm inclined to agree with her. You do have an untouched look which I don't think my wife should have. I'll have to do something about it. Siesta is as good a time as any.'

Now both his hands were on her shoulders. Warm and possessive, they slipped across her back as he pulled her towards him.

'No, Max,' she whispered. Head back, she put her hands flat against his chest to push him away, hoping he could not hear the excited beating of her heart, keeping her eyelids lowered in case he saw fear leaping in her eyes.

'You said that very uncertainly, as if you didn't mean it,' he mocked, his mouth so close to hers that she felt his breath waft across her lips. 'You know, I'm beginning to think your problem arises from the fact that we haven't been practising lately. Perhaps this is the way we should have been passing the time when we've been alone together.'

She pushed against him with all her strength. The hard bones and muscles of his chest were like a wall of steel, inflexible, making her efforts seem puny. Whoever had said women are equal to men had got it all wrong, she thought a little wildly. She didn't have a chance in a struggle like this.

She continued to push and twist, not because she didn't want him to kiss her but because she was afraid of what his kiss might do to her in her present vulnerable state of mind and body, there in the somnolent silence of the lovely room.

Gradually she realised that her resistance was not having any effect; he was not withdrawing at all. In fact he was holding her more tightly, and once again she felt the cruel strength of his fingers as he gripped her upper arms and flung her back against the hump of pillows at the head of the bed.

'You can fight all you want, little firebrand, but you're not going to get away now,' he growled at her.

She had a brief glimpse of his face, no longer stolid and impassive but alive with devilry, the light eyes seeming to blaze with pale flame. The sleeping devil had burst forth, but in an entirely different way and for an entirely different reason from what she had expected. And instead of fire and brimstone there was the heat and breathlessness of a passion which she had inadvertently aroused by her resistance to him. Fear and pain made her cry out in an attempt to divert him from his obvious intention.

'Brute!' she accused. But he only laughed at her, his teeth flashing white against his sun-darkened face.

Anger lent her new strength and once more she struggled to free herself from the hands which were holding her down against the softness of the bed. She almost escaped, only to find he had caught her back with an arm lock. Twisting within that hold, she managed to bite his brawny forearm and felt a heady triumph when she heard him grunt with pain. But triumph was short-lived because in retaliation he slapped her, a light blow with his fingers that stung her cheek and made her go limp with amazement and outraged pride.

'You hit me!' she accused shakily, glaring up at him.

'You bit me,' he retorted. 'And now I'm going to kiss you whether you want me to or not.'

Again Lee twisted her head to avoid the kiss, so he kissed the tender curve where her neck sloped into her shoulder. He went on from there and, trapped by his weight, feeling his kisses leave a trail of fire on her soft sensitive skin so that she longed suddenly to put her arms round him and cradle his head against her, Lee realised that he was offering her temptations which she no longer wanted to resist.

But if she didn't resist, what would happen? Passion might sweep them both into a course of action which later they might regret. It was only fair to remind him, because her instinct suggested that he would hate to be the one who broke the rules of any contract he had signed.

135

'Max, remember the condition,' she whispered breathlessly.

He lay quite still for a moment and the only sounds in the warm sun-slatted room were their breathing, quickened by the passion which had flared unexpectedly between them and the dull thudding of their hearts. Then he moved away from her, freeing her to lie on his side, his elbow denting the pillow, his head supported by his hand as he looked down at her.

She didn't move because any movement might set him in action again, but she flinched a little as he raised his other hand to lift a swathe of her bright hair and wind his fingers in it.

'When I set out to kiss you it wasn't my intention to break that condition,' he murmured, 'and whether it is broken or not this afternoon depends entirely on you.' He paused, and his mouth curved in a rueful smile as he gave her hair a gentle tug. 'I like the spitfire temper which goes with this hair,' he went on, 'but your refusal to do as I ask, your resistance to me just now, only roused my own devil of a temper and made me more determined to get my own way. I want you to wear that necklace. I want you to look kissed and possessed as anybody knowing me would expect my wife to look.'

He leaned over her again. His mouth hovered tantalisingly above hers. The firm lips were no longer thinned in control but were slightly parted so that she saw the glint of his teeth behind them. His hand was now firmly wound in her hair and any attempt to escape would only bring her further pain. But she didn't want to escape any more.

'What are you going to do, *lieveling*?' His voice made music soft and hypnotic, lulling her fears.

'I'll wear the necklace.' Agreement brought a lovely sense of release and as tension eased out of her all sorts of new exciting sensations took over, cravings which she had been trying to ignore and keep under control for days.

He kissed her immediately, a long lingering caress, the sweetness of which drew from her an involuntary yet passionate response, so that when he raised his head again he found himself being held closely by her hands which had crept round his neck. She was too close to see his eyes together, so she studied them one at a time. Each one was the colour of warm grey smoke and their expression was quizzical.

'What's this?' he asked in a surprise-shaken voice. 'An invitation to stay and share your siesta with you?'

'Please stay,' she murmured shyly, obeying the messages which her body was sending out, doing what she had been wanting to do for some time; touching with a tender finger-tip the edges of the thick fans of lashes which rimmed his eyes, stroking one strangely peaked eyebrow, spreading out her fingers to tangle them in his hair, then raising her head a little to touch with her mouth the curve at the corner of his mouth.

'To hell with conditions,' he muttered gruffly, and as his mouth came down over hers, forcing her lips open, bruising their tenderness against her teeth, joy flared up in a spurt of bright flame to illuminate the darker flames of passion and to colour everything that happened in that room of afternoon somnolence, making it right.

CHAPTER SIX

SOFT light shed from a shimmering crystal chandelier gleamed on the red, blue and white of the chips which were set out on the black cloth of the roulette table. In the centre of the table the wooden disc which was marked in black and red revolved quickly. Four silvery pointers in the middle which had set it in motion glittered with sparks of light and the little ivory ball which was hopping about the sides of the disc clattered gaily; click, click, click. It was the only noise in the room where that most genteel and relaxed of all gambling games was being played.

Most of the gamblers were women, seated round the table watching with bated breath as the revolutions slowed down, waiting for the little ball to find a home in one of the red or black compartments, hoping that the home it chose would be the number on which they had wagered their chips. For a few moments the silence was tense, and the laughter and conversation coming from the other rooms in the hotel's casino seemed to mock that silence.

Her copper-coloured hair piled in shining coils on top of her head, showing off the slender column of her neck around which the necklace of gold and emeralds glowed with mysterious bluish-green fire, her slim body swathed in a sea-green gown cut on Grecian lines which left one of her creamy-skinned shoulders bare, Lee watched the centre intently.

Several times she had been lucky that evening. If she won again, according to her rough mental calculations she would win enough to pay back to Max the money with which he had staked her the first night she had played, and would also have quite a large amount over to add to her winnings of the previous two nights' play. Enough to pay the air-fare back to Amsterdam.

The possibility of winning enough money to pay that fare and so becoming independent of Max had suggested itself to her the first time she had been successful. She did not question it, but accepted it as something she must do in case of need at some future date.

Max was standing behind her now, wearing conventional black and white. She knew just how he would look, solid yet suave, one hand in a pocket of his white tuxedo jacket, the other holding a half-smoked after-dinner cigar as he also watched the centre piece, and she was aware in every nerve of her body of each move he made and each breath he took.

She had been like this ever since siesta time two days ago; ever since that hour of joy-lit passion. It had not been repeated because they had been too involved in fun and entertainment provided by the hotel to indulge in siesta again, and their nights had ended only when dancing finished in the early hours of the morning and she had been glad to sink into slumber in the big beautiful room. But she was on the alert all the time, half hoping that it would happen.

The centre stopped turning. The little ball fell into a compartment. A chorus of groans muffled with laughter came from the people seated round the table, but Lee clapped her hands in unaffected delight. The number was hers! She had won again, and the croupier was raking in the chips and pushing them towards her with a smile.

'Enough is enough,' said Max from behind. 'Quit now while you're winning, and let's go and dance.'

They collected up the chips and went to cash them. Max thrust the money into her hand. Meticulously she separated the amount he had given her for her original stake, and offered it to him.

'Keep it,' he said curtly.

'No. I should really give you all I've won because I couldn't have played at all if you hadn't staked me,' she argued. 'Please take it. If you don't I'll go and buy some more chips and play until I've lost every guilder.'

His mouth twitched with amusement.

'And you know how much that would irritate my thrifty mind,' he replied. 'All right, I'll take it.'

They moved together, a tall distinguished black-haired, olive-skinned man and a slender auburn-haired, creamy-skinned young woman, drawing the attention of many of the people who thronged the rooms of the casino through which they passed on their way to the lobby of the hotel.

'Hello, Max, how are you? It's good to see you.'

The voice, a husky contralto, spoke in Dutch. It went with brassy blonde hair which was waved back from a strong-featured face made attractive by a smooth golden tan and a gay white smile. A tall full-breasted figure was outlined by a simple black gown, high-necked, straight-skirted and sleeveless, revealing long graceful golden arms.

'Hello, Beatrix.' Max spoke in English and it was difficult to tell whether he was pleased or surprised.

'You must be Lee,' said the woman, also speaking English with a pronounced American accent. She held out a hand to Lee, who felt the full effects of the brilliant friendly smile which made light blue eyes crinkle attractively at the corners, giving the whole face an expression of jollity. 'I'm Beatrix Deering. My mother told me that Max had a child bride.' The blue eyes flickered observantly over Lee's slender but well-shaped figure. 'You look all woman to me,' she added with an attractive throaty chuckle which robbed the words of any offence.

'She is. I can vouch for that,' said Max, and as he slipped his arm possessively round her Lee felt the colour rising

140

warmly in her cheeks at his oblique suggestion that their marriage had its physical side.

'Lee, I'd like you to meet Tiede De Boer,' Beatrix was saying, gesturing to the tall thin man who was standing beside her and who was staring at Lee as if he couldn't believe his eyes. He extended his hand and murmured in a gruff guttural voice that he was very pleased to meet her.

'What are you doing here, Tiede?' Max asked. 'I thought you never left that office of yours if you could help it.'

'Beatrix's idea,' replied the man with a grin and a shrug of his high narrow shoulders.

'Tiede is acting as my lawyer,' Beatrix said, facing up to Max. She was almost as tall as he was, Lee noticed, and found herself wondering what sort of messages were passing between blue eyes and grey ones and back again as the two stared at each other.

'Sounds ominous,' murmured Max with a grin. 'Why should you bring your lawyer here with you?'

'To talk to you about the takeover bid the Van Breedan Company has made for Volney's Gifts Ltd. When I returned to Willemstad last week I hoped to find you there. Then someone . . .'

'Your mother,' suggested Max wickedly.

'No, as a matter of fact Cora de Palm, your secretary, told me you had got married. Later Mother told me she had heard you were coming to Aruba, so I looked up Tiede and persuaded him to come here to see the carnival parade. We called on Irene this morning and she told us where we would find you.'

'And no doubt told you all there is to know as well,' said Max with a touch of irony.

'Yes, she told me everything,' replied Beatrix. The good humour had faded from her face and she gave Lee a long assessing glance. Then she turned back to Max. 'I thought you and I might be able to get together for half an hour and thrash out the whole business of the takeover before the deadline,' she added briskly.

'Maybe we can, but not tonight,' replied Max coolly. 'Lee and I have a date to go dancing.'

'Then tomorrow,' urged Beatrix brightly, refusing to be put off. 'Why not mix business with pleasure, Max? It won't be the first time you've done that.' Again she chuckled, as if she shared secrets with him of which Lee could not possibly have any knowledge.

'No, it won't,' he agreed equably, 'but this time is different. This time I'm on my honeymoon.'

Lee, as sensitive as ever, quivered in reaction to that cruel thrust as if it had been intended for her and not for Beatrix, but Beatrix did not turn a hair.

'How careless of me to forget,' she exclaimed. 'Forgive me, both of you.' The warm winning smile was once more directed at Lee, who could not help smiling back as she admired the other woman's poise. 'Then let's all go and dance. Coming, Tiede?'

'You know I don't dance,' he replied, with a long-suffering sigh and an expression of comical dismay that made Lee laugh.

'Yes, I know,' said Beatrix, pushing a hand through his lax arm and urging him forward towards the room where dancing and cabaret were held every night. 'But you'll enjoy watching everyone else dancing.'

As she sat at one of the tables which were set round the edge of the dance floor, Lee sipped the drink Max had ordered for her and tried to hear what Beatrix was saying to him. It was difficult because of the noise of the music, and because the woman was sitting on the other side of him, but she gathered the conversation was about Beatrix's return to her home town and the mutual acquaintances of hers and Max's that she had run into.

'And only yesterday I saw that young man I met when I

142

was last in town and called on Bruno.' Was it her imagination, Lee wondered, or was the husky voice louder than it had been? Certainly every word was now carrying clearly across the table to her.

'Which young man?' asked Max idly.

'The one with the blond hair and blue eyes, the most handsome creature on two legs I've ever seen. I think his name is Adrian something.'

'Where did you see him?' Beneath the apparent casualness of the question Lee detected the cold inquisitorial approach Max had used on her when they had first met. She could feel her face going taut and pale, although she tried to appear unconcerned as she watched the dancers circling the floor.

'On Heerenstraat. We met face to face. I was just going to speak to him when he rushed past me and disappeared. Doesn't he work for the company any more?' said Beatrix.

'No.' Max's voice was curt as his hand sought Lee's under the cover of the table. 'Come and dance,' he murmured.

She was grateful for the warm clasp of his hand on hers as he led her on the floor, and glad that the music being played was slow and sentimental, so that it was the most natural thing in the world to slip into his arms and to dance as others were dancing, closely, cheek to cheek.

After a while he said quietly,

'Are you all right?' Once before he had asked her the same question; so long ago, it seemed, in his office when she had almost blacked out after he had told her Adrian had probably left Willemstad. Now she knew that sincere concern lay behind the laconic words.

'Yes, thank you.'

'She could have been mistaken, you know,' he went on. 'It might not have been him. There are lots of young men with blond hair and blue eyes.'

Lee knew that to be true because many times her heart had leapt with hope at the glimpse of a blond head in a crowd and she had hurried to see if it belonged to Adrian, only to experience a sad and sinking feeling of disappointment when she had discovered it belonged to a stranger.

'I know. It never *is* him,' she replied, her voice plaintive as a result of remembered disappointment.

Max was silent, but gradually she realised he had pushed her away from him, so that they were dancing in a more conventional fashion, slightly apart so that he could look down and see the expression on her face, clearly revealed in spite of the dimness of the lighting.

'Does that mean you haven't stopped looking for him?' he asked, his voice crisp.

She wished he would hold her closely again. It would be so much easier to lie to him if he were not watching her.

'Yes,' she whispered honestly.

He didn't ask any more questions and he didn't hold her closely again. The music came to an end and they returned to the table. Beatrix and Tiede had been joined by two other couples who also knew Max; more drinks were ordered, and the conversation was light and gay, controlled always by the sparkling-eyed vivacious Beatrix, whose lively, slightly earthy sense of humour set them all laughing.

The cabaret performers appeared on the small stage; an American blues singer with shining ebony skin, swathed in glittering sequins and feathers; an audacious group of South American guitarists wearing full-sleeved silk shirts, tight black pants and coloured sombreros; a comedian with his rather dumb blonde girl sidekick; and last but not least, a group from Curaçao who performed a *tambue*, a song and dance to the beat of a drum, the two men dressed in suits made from flour bags, the two women wearing gaily printed flounced dresses.

When the cabaret was over the dancing started again.

Max asked Beatrix to dance, the other couples teamed up and Lee found herself alone with Tiede. For a while she watched Max and Beatrix. They looked well together, his darkness complementing her blondeness, and they talked and laughed as they danced, moving with the ease of people who knew each other well and who had often danced together.

Lee felt a sudden sharp pang. She wished it was herself who was out there in Beatrix's place. Confused by the painful feeling which was new, she looked away and found that Tiede was watching her, a slightly mocking expression on his long sallow face.

'I wonder if you realise what a great shock Max's marriage to you has been to Beatrix,' he said, moving round to sit in the chair next to her.

She wasn't quite sure how to answer the question. How much was she supposed to know? If it hadn't been for that unfortunate meeting with Sophy Volney, Beatrix's mother, she would have known nothing—and so perhaps would have not been so uncomfortable at the sight of Max dancing with Beatrix, the woman from whom he had been inseparable at one time.

'I don't see why it should have been more of a shock to her than it was to anyone else,' she parried.

Tiede's tired brown eyes smiled at her.

'No, of course you don't. I was forgetting you were not around at the time so you wouldn't know. In fact I realise now that when Max and Beatrix were going about together some ten years ago, you were only a child, a schoolgirl.'

This time the strange pang of pain was sharper and Lee had difficulty in not showing how much his remarks hurt her.

'We all expected them to marry,' continued Tiede, 'it would have been an important liaison between two well-known business families: but, as in the case of Romeo and

Juliet, parental interference and bad timing decreed otherwise.'

Lee was silent, her glance going again to Beatrix's bright head close to Max's dark one as they danced. Romeo and Juliet, now mature and experienced, worldly-wise. Had their love survived?

'But *she* married someone else, so why should she be shocked just because *he's* married?' she asked, turning back to Tiede.

'A good question,' he replied, as he lit a cigar. 'Why indeed? Because she believed, or was led to believe by other people who discussed such matters, that he had remained a bachelor because he had found no one to replace her in his life. As a result of her belief, a few months ago, before Eric Deering was taken ill, she filed a divorce petition on the grounds of incompatibility. She came back to Willemstad to tell Max, but he was away again in England, sailing in a racing dinghy championship. By the time he returned home she was back in the States, called to her husband's sick-bed.'

'When did her husband die?' Lee asked numbly.

'He lingered, keeping her there, and died a month ago. She had a terrible time trying to settle his debts and arrived back in Willemstad a week ago. She admits her timing was bad, but then she had no reason to believe that Max was considering marriage to another woman. None of us had.'

Here it was again, the insinuation that there was something odd about Max's marriage because he had married in secret a young woman no one had ever seen before. How should she deal with it? Tiede was a lawyer, trained to dig information out of people and to assess the answers they gave him, to find the germ of truth in a lie.

'No one could have been more surprised than I was when Max asked me to marry him,' she answered truthfully.

146

'He's very good at concealing his real feelings, and so when he does something he wants to do very badly he surprises everyone.'

The brown eyes studied her intently. A gleam crept into them and Tiede smiled slowly.

'You seem to have great understanding of him,' he murmured, 'and I congratulate you on your reply. Now I'm going to tell you one of my secrets, which you'll keep to yourself, I hope.'

'Yes, I will,' she said, suddenly liking him. Plain in appearance he might be, dry as dust in the way he spoke, but she sensed he was kind and had a concern for other people.

'I am probably one of the few people who know both Beatrix and Max and the way they used to be, who is glad he is married at last to you and not to her.'

Lee's eyes widened in surprise as she stared at him.

'You mean you're in love with her?' she gasped.

'I am. I love her dearly and have done for a few years,' he admitted with a self-mocking, crooked grin.

'Oh, but supposing ...' Lee began, then broke off. To tell Tiede what she suspected, that Max and Beatrix were still in love with each other, would be to reveal the truth, that Max had married her for convenience.

'Supposing what?' he prompted, watching her closely.

'Nothing.' She forced herself to smile. 'I wish you luck.'

'Thank you.' His voice was dry again as he leaned back in his chair and watched the dancers. 'Watching Beatrix in action tonight I think I'm going to need every bit of luck I can get.' He shot a sharp glance at her. 'And so are you,' he added rather grimly.

There was no chance for her to ask him why she needed luck too, because the others were returning to the table, but the remark stayed with Lee like a warning as she found herself watching, not Beatrix, but Max. For the first time

147

since they had been married he ignored her in public, seeming to be much more interested in talking to Beatrix. It was true he danced with her again several times, but he did not hold her closely, and she had the impression he was dancing with her only because it was important to show anyone who was interested that Max Van Breedan and his new wife danced together and there was nothing lacking in their relationship.

The night wore on. Lee felt her eyes beginning to smart from the haze of smoke, her head beginning to ache in reaction to the noise of rock music. She saw Max lean towards Beatrix and whisper something in her ear, saw the woman laugh and tap his cheek lightly with her fingers in an intimate gesture, perhaps in joking reprimand for what he had said.

Suddenly Lee could stand no more. Rising to her feet, she excused herself to the others. Max looked up and rose to his feet too.

'Tired?' he asked as she went to him.

'Yes. Very. You don't have to come up with me.'

His eyes glinted with annoyance as his hand took hold of her arm above the elbow.

'I do have to come. It's in the rules,' he jibed softly.

'We'll see you both tomorrow?' That was Beatrix's voice raised in query. 'At the pool, bright and early for a pre-breakfast swim, Lee? Later we can all watch the parade together.'

'Yes, yes, that will be nice. Goodnight.' Lee was smiling even though her head felt as if it would split in two at any moment.

In the elevator they didn't speak. Max leaned against the back wall and watched the lighted indicator. His face was impassive, taut and dark, the eyes hidden, and she guessed he was deep in thought. His withdrawal baffled her. She missed the warmth and friendliness he had shown recently, and she could only blame it on the arrival of Beatrix. But she was too tired to ask questions. The late nights, the high emotional level on which she had been living for the last few days, had finally caught up with her. She longed for sleep.

He unlocked the door of the big bedroom and she went past him into the room. He switched on the light as he always did, and glanced round to make sure all was well, but as usual he did not stay.

'I'll see you tomorrow. Goodnight, sleep well,' he said, as he had said every night since they had been married.

She replied, and the door closed. Alone, she stared at the wooden panelling as she fought with an impulse to fling the door wide open, to shout after him, to ask him where he was going, for she felt sure he was not going to his own room. But to give in to such an impulse would be to break the rules, to behave like a real wife; and she was only a bargain bride, a makeshift wife whom he had married in an emergency because the woman he should have married had not been available at the time when he needed to marry.

Sighing, Lee turned towards the dressing table and unclasped the necklace. As she laid it in its box she could not help thinking that by rights Beatrix should have been wearing it; by rights Beatrix should be in this room, and if she were she would not have been left to sleep alone.

Dragging her thoughts back from that dangerous direction, she pondered on the amazing piece of information Beatrix had passed on that evening; her accidental meeting with Adrian in the street. Could the woman have made a mistake? After all, she had met Adrian only once, so she might have done. But if she hadn't, if he were still there in Willemstad, could he be found? Again Lee sighed, and slid her nightdress over her head. She would like to see Adrian again if only to lay a ghost, she thought sadly, the ghost of her love for him.

She slept almost as soon as her head touched the pillow, and woke next morning with a feeling she had slept later than usual. A glance at the digital clock on the bedside table confirmed this, so she sprang out of bed and padded to the communicating door, knocked on it, opened the door and looked into the other bedroom. The big bed was unmade, and Max's black silk pyjamas were lying on it where they had been tossed. There was no sign of him. Probably he had gone for his usual morning swim in the surf but had not yet returned. Because he had been waylaid by Beatrix?

The idea winged into her mind from nowhere, and before she realised it she was out on the balcony where she and Max had breakfasted together ever since they had arrived at the hotel. Leaning on the wrought-iron railings, she looked down at the blue rectangle of the swimming pool. No one was swimming in it and it was impossible from this height to see whether anyone was sitting under the shade of the striped umbrellas which cast shade over loungers and deck chairs set about the concrete apron.

Lee hurried back into her own room and dressed quickly in a dark green bikini. She pulled on a straight, brightly-coloured beach robe, stepped into white cork-soled sandals, pushed towel and swimming cap into a beach bag, slung it over one shoulder and made for the elevator which would take her to the ground floor.

As soon as she stepped through the wide patio doors on to the apron which surrounded the pool, she heard the sound of Beatrix's voice. It came from the other side of the pool, and Lee found her there. Her blonde hair glinting, her long golden legs revealed by the short skirt of a blue and white swimsuit, the deeply plunging bodice of which showed a fair amount of golden-hued breasts, she was lying on a lounger and talking to a stranger who was also making the most of the morning sun to improve her suntan.

As soon as Beatrix saw Lee she smiled gaily.

'Hi! I was wondering what had happened to you,' she said. 'Where's Max?'

He wasn't there after all, and judging from her question Beatrix hadn't seen him.

'I ... he ... we overslept,' Lee said vaguely. 'I hurried down. I was afraid you might think we'd forgotten we said we'd see you here.'

'That was nice of you,' Beatrix smiled again. 'Then you haven't had breakfast?'

'No.'

'Neither have I. Shall we have it together in the coffee shop? It will give us a chance to get to know one another.' Beatrix rose to her feet and excused herself pleasantly to the stranger. She slipped on an elegant black and white beach robe, gathered up her beach bag, and taking Lee's arm in a friendly fashion began to walk towards the hotel.

'You know, as one of Max's oldest friends I feel I should be a friend of his wife,' she went on in a low husky voice. 'At first, when I heard that he had married you I wanted to shut you out, close my mind to you. I didn't want to admit your existence.' She laughed, rather self-deprecatingly, and hugged Lee's arm against her. 'Silly of me, wasn't it, because if I didn't I would forfeit Max's friendship, and I don't want to do that. Do you think you and I can be friends, Lee? Or am I expecting too much, as usual?'

'We could try,' replied Lee, unable to resist the disarming appeal to her good nature.

In the coffee shop they sat at a table for two and ate scrambled eggs and drank delicious hot coffee. Beatrix talked; she seemed to enjoy talking, and told Lee a little about her late husband.

'He was one of those charming men who know all the right things to say to a woman to make her feel she is needed, and when I met him I was in a bad way. I was just

151

recovering from a love affair which had gone awry.' Beatrix paused and fidgeted with the cutlery, and Lee guessed that the love affair had been with Max. 'Eric came along. He was on holiday recuperating from a bad car smash in which his first wife had been killed. We went about together, he proposed to me and I accepted. My parents were furious.' Beatrix's mouth took a downward turn. 'I've often thought since that if they hadn't opposed me so much I might not have married Eric. But their opposition fanned the flame of rebellion, and when Eric flew out of Curaçao on a plane bound for Miami I was with him.'

'Were you happy with him?' Lee asked.

'For a while, yes, because he gave me everything I wanted regardless of cost, but it wasn't long before I ran into the difficulties a woman always has to face when she marries a man who is very much older than she is. Eric was twenty-five years older than I, and often when I wanted to be gay and go dancing he wanted nothing more than to sit at home and put his feet up. But I liked the way of life in the city where we lived and he was very generous. And now he has gone, leaving me without any visible means of support.'

There was a little silence. Lee wasn't sure what to say, whether she should express sympathy or change the subject. Before she could make up her mind, Beatrix leaned forward and said in a conspiratorial way:

'Lee, you've got to help me.'

'What can I do?' asked Lee, her eyes opening wide.

'Give me half an hour of Max's time. You see, it's very important that I stop the takeover of my father's old business by the Van Breedan Company. It's due to happen next week. Now that Eric is dead I have to work for my living, and I would prefer to work for myself in the business in which I grew up. Do you understand?'

'Yes, I think so. You want to keep control over the gift

shops and you'd like to discuss the problem with Max here.'

'That's right. Only you heard him last night. He's on his honeymoon.' There was a touch of bitterness in the husky voice. 'So I was wondering if you would mind very much if I took up a little of his time during the next few days ... possibly when we're all together, swimming or sightseeing. If I could just get him to myself for half an hour I'm sure I could get him to delay the takeover.'

What should she say? How could she refuse such an appeal? Warnings were jangling in Lee's mind, but to refuse Beatrix's request would seem mean, small-minded, possibly over-jealous.

'I can't really stop you from talking to Max,' she said with a little laugh. 'I've no objection.'

'Thank you, dear, I knew you'd understand.' Beatrix's voice was huskier than ever with emotion and tears actually glinted in her eyes. 'Oh, look, there's Tiede, poor soul. He looks lost. Between you and me, Lee, he hates hotels. I had a terrible time persuading him to come. Hello, Tiede. Sleep well?'

'Well, but not enough,' sighed Tiede, sliding into a chair at the next table. 'Now, what little plot are you hatching with Lee?'

'No plot, just coming to an understanding. Lee is very understanding. What time does the parade begin?'

'In about half an hour, I believe.'

'I must find Max,' Lee muttered, rising to her feet.

'We'll see you both in the lobby. We might as well all go together to the parade,' Beatrix called after her.

Max hadn't returned to the suite, and by the time she had showered and dressed in one of the pretty cotton dresses he had chosen for her Lee was worried. This was the first time in nearly three weeks that they had not breakfasted together, and even though he had often gone off on his own when they had stayed at the bungalow, she had always known where he might be. Now she had no idea. To go down to the lobby and meet Beatrix and Tiede without Max was going to look strange, but she didn't know what else she should do, so when the lift doors opened and she stepped into the lobby and saw him standing beside Beatrix, listening to something the woman was saying, relief rushed through Lee, crowding out any other feeling.

As she approached he looked up and gave her a bright searching glance. She smiled at him. He did not smile back, but turned to say something to Beatrix. The cold blankness of his stare, the way he had looked away from her without smiling, gave her a shock. Then she told herself not to be silly; possibly Beatrix had been talking to him about the takeover and he was thinking about it, hardly aware that Lee was there.

She went up to him and tucked her hand through the crook of his arm in the usual way to show the others she had a right to do that. He did not shake it off, but she felt his muscles tauten under her fingers as if he resented that little gesture of possession.

A little bewildered, feeling instinctively that something was wrong, Lee was glad that the colour and excitement of the parade absorbed her attention for the next hour. Dressed in costumes which represented the many cultures from which the inhabitants of the islands were descended, hundreds of young people thronged the streets following the decorated floats.

Dutch girls in wide stiff skirts, tulip-shaped caps and wooden clogs danced along beside Spanish *señoritas* in flounced skirts, white blouses and elegant shawls. Dutch boys in flat blue caps and baggy pants rubbed shoulders with matadors in tight-fitting breeches, frilly shirts, short jaunty jackets and stiff black sombreros. Other traditional costumes were represented as Chinese mandarins shuffled past and a group of Indonesians cavorted by in a ritual dance.

And everywhere there was the sound of music; the hollow metallic ring of steel drums, the brassy blare of trumpets, the thin shrill sound of flutes and the inevitable strumming of guitars.

As if at a signal the people in the parade invaded the bystanders, inviting them to dance. Lee found herself being swung off her feet by a huge man dressed in the traditional costume of a slave, a white suit made from flour bags, the jacket tied at the waist by a scarlet tie belt.

When at last he released her and went on his way, his big white teeth shining in his dark face, she was a long way from Max and the others and it took her some time to rejoin them as she struggled against the tide of laughing, singing people.

The dancing and the merrymaking lasted all day in some form or other, and for Lee it culminated in a party at the house of Irene and Claus which was attended by many of Claus's friends and acquaintances from the refinery. It was well past midnight when she and Max, accompanied by Beatrix and Tiede, at last returned to the hotel.

Again she slept heavily and wakened late, knowing instinctively that Max had gone swimming and had not returned to share breakfast with her. Stifling a pang of disappointment because he did not seem to want to be alone with her at all now, she ordered breakfast for herself and ate it sitting at the round table on the balcony, alone except for the bananaquits, the plump yellow-bellied birds that flew in as usual to raid the sugar and the marmalade.

By the time she had finished the meal Max had not come back, so she went down to the lobby and wandered out to the beach, that perfect crescent of soft silken sand which rimmed the sparkling greenish-blue water.

Shading her hands against the glare of sunlight on sand

and sea Lee looked about her, searching for Max. The beach was empty: no one was swimming in the tumbling waves. She decided to go back to the hotel. A movement at the far end of the beach where it curved to meet a rocky point of land caught her attention, and she shaded her eyes again to stare.

Sunlight glinted on bright brassy blonde hair. *Beatrix!* and she wasn't alone. Beside her walked a tall broad-shouldered figure, solid, with long muscular legs revealed by short swimming trunks. *Max.*

So Beatrix had managed to get her half hour alone with him. They were walking slowly back from the point. Then Beatrix put a hand on Max's arm; he stopped and turned to her. For a moment they faced each other, tall, well-matched, like equal halves of a whole, their figures dark against the bright sand stretching beyond them.

They were talking business, that was all, but even as she reminded herself Lee saw the two figures blend one with the other in a close embrace.

'No!' Lee was not aware of shouting the word aloud as if in denial of what her eyes could see. Not wanting to see any more, she whirled and ran back across the soft yielding sand to the hotel, blundering blindly into people and apologising as she ran.

In the lobby hands caught at her and held her firmly. She looked up into a thin sallow face in which brown eyes were narrowing shrewdly.

'You're in a hurry. Where are you going?' growled Tiede.

'I forgot something. I'm ... just going back to my room to get it,' she stumbled evasively.

'The lifts are in the other direction,' he said dryly, and she avoided his glance.

'Where are *you* going?' she countered.

'To look for Beatrix, of course.' His faint smile mocked himself.

'She's on the beach with Max. They're talking business.' She was pleased with the sound of her voice. It sounded cool and steady.

'Naturally, and you being a nice understanding child have left them alone for a while,' he murmured. His hands fell from her arms. Raising a hand, he pinched his lower lip between thumb and forefinger while he gazed at her consideringly. 'Has Max taken you to see the caves on the north side of the island yet?'

'No, he hasn't. We've only been to Ayó to see the diorite rocks.'

'Ah, yes, the ones which have been formed into weird shapes by the action of the weather,' Tiede nodded.

'I thought they looked like toys belonging to a giant baby, that he'd thrown down in a tantrum,' said Lee, determined to act normally and ignore the painful thoughts concerning Max and Beatrix.

'A good description,' said Tiede. 'Would you like to see the caves?'

'Are they interesting?'

'To me they are. They have signs on their walls which were painted long ago by the Arawak Indians. It would give me great pleasure to take you to see them now.'

'This morning?' It would be something to do and most of all it would show she had no intention of hanging around waiting for Max while he had a business conference with the woman he should have married.

'Yes, we could hire a car and drive over. We'll leave a message for the others to say we'll be back for lunch. What do you say? Would you like to go?'

'Yes, I would,' Lee answered gratefully.

So the message was left and the car was hired, and soon they were driving in the direction of Orenjestad. Just before they reached the town they took a turning to the left on to a road which angled inland, crossing the barren land where only cacti grew among the coral-covered rock. The road deteriorated into a narrow track and soon the sea, shimmering under the sun, came into view again.

The car was left at the top of the amber-coloured limestone cliffs, and following a path well-worn by tourists they found their way to the entrance of one of the caves, a huge grotto full of glimmering sea-light by which Lee could make out the signs which had been painted on the roof.

'The Indians probably thought of the ceiling as the vault of heaven,' Tiede explained. 'As you can see, many of the symbols are like the sun or the stars and even the moon, but on the walls here you can see pictures of animals. Look, here is a snake. There is a lizard. Reproduction of animals in pictures or in paintings is typical of all the tribes that originally inhabited both South America and North America and these islands of the Caribbean.'

They lingered for a while in the cave as Tiede gave her the benefit of the historical and geographical knowledge he had acquired. The cliffs, it seemed, were honeycombed with passages linking one cave to another, and they were going down one of the labyrinthine passages when they heard footsteps behind them and then Beatrix's voice calling to them. Tiede answered, and within minutes Max and Beatrix had joined them in another high-ceilinged rocky room, gouged out of the rock by the action of the sea long years ago.

The meeting was natural, without strain. Max and Beatrix had received Tiede's message and, since Beatrix had never visited the caves either, they had decided to follow. After exclaiming at the height and depth of the cave, at the strange signs painted on its walls, Beatrix expressed a desire to explore further and urged Tiede to go with her along another passage.

Lee moved to go after them, but was detained by Max's hand on her arm.

'Why did you come here with Tiede?' he asked, his voice

158

cold, expressing such disapproval that she looked up in surprise. In the uncertain light of the cave his face looked rather grim and his eyes were tired, with dark lines under them as if he had slept little.

'He invited me, and I thought it would be a good way of filling in time. I knew you were with Beatrix, talking business. She asked me yesterday if I would mind if she could have half an hour with you, and I agreed. When I saw you walking with her on the beach I supposed that she was having her half-hour.'

'I see,' he drawled, and there was a steely glint in his eyes which warned her he was not pleased. 'So you think you can make appointments for me, do you? Better watch your step. That isn't part of your job and I don't like it when someone else tries to organise my life.'

'Oh, I didn't, I wasn't trying to organise anything,' she spluttered. What had Beatrix told him? That his wife had suggested he would be free for half an hour this morning on the beach? 'Oh, Max, please can we go home to-morrow?' she added, although she had had no idea of making the suggestion a few minutes earlier. It had just come to her that away from Aruba they would be away from Beatrix.

'Home?' he repeated, raising his eyebrows in surprise. 'Where is that for you?'

How cruel he could be, she thought miserably, and his face blurred as tears rushed to her eyes. Where indeed was home for her now? Whatever had given her the idea that it would be wherever he lived?

'I meant can we go back to Curaçao, to Willemstad,' she muttered.

'Don't you like it here? I thought people, entertainment, were what you wanted. I thought you didn't want to be alone too much with me,' he countered coldly.

'I . . . it was what I wanted . . . only now . . .' she faltered

159

to a stop, unable to explain her confused feelings.

'Only now you would rather be in Willemstad,' he said with a touch of weariness, as if he were tired of whims. 'All right, we'll fly back tomorrow. After all, the week is nearly ended and the honeymoon time is almost over.' His irony had a sharp bite and Lee could not help but flinch in reaction, but he didn't notice because he had turned away from her as if to follow the others.

There was something wrong, something terribly wrong, and she had to find out what it was. It was her turn to detain him by reaching out and putting a hand on his arm. He turned to her at once and again she was struck by the signs of strain on his face.

'Max, is something the matter?' she asked tentatively.

'Why do you ask?' he parried, his face becoming impassive, his eyes cold and expressionless.

'You ... you've ... I ...' He had withdrawn from her, too far for her to be able to say what she wanted to say. But she had to make an effort to cross the invisible barrier which seemed to have reared up between them. 'Everything has been so different since Beatrix and Tiede came, and I was wondering if perhaps you're wishing that you hadn't married me in such a hurry,' she managed to say at last.

He stared at her for a moment, his dark eyebrows pulled together in a frown. Then his eyelids dropped and his face took on that dark secretive look which meant he wasn't going to tell her how he felt.

'I have no regrets,' he said in a cold clipped voice. 'Nothing has changed. You're my wife and I want you to continue to remember that, especially in public. Next time another man invites you to accompany him on an outing in the way that Tiede invited you today, you will refuse.'

The cold autocratic speech cut through Lee's bewilderment and sparked off her temper. She snatched her hand from his arm.

'You mean I mustn't break any rules,' she retorted, 'and I mustn't object when you break any, I suppose.'

Even in the dim light of the cave she saw the lightning flash of his eyes when he looked up.

'I'm not aware that I've broken any, at least not without your full agreement,' he said icily, and at this oblique reference to what had happened between them at siesta time five days ago, her cheeks flamed.

'You went walking this morning with another woman on the beach, which is a public place,' she flared, hurt beyond endurance by his jibe, 'yet I mustn't accept an invitation from another man. I suppose you're afraid I might create a scandal like Bruno's wife, if I behave independently or do my own thing. And that mustn't happen, must it? No breath of scandal must touch the name of Van Breedan . . .' She broke off with a gasp, because he had gripped her arms and his fingers bit into the flesh cruelly.

'Be quiet! You might be heard. These caves echo,' he warned her.

'And that would be terrible, wouldn't it, if anyone heard the wife of the respectable Max Van Breedan telling him a few home truths!' she flung at him recklessly.

'Listen to me, you little fire-eater,' he said, giving her a sharp shake. 'You've forgotten you made an appointment for me with Beatrix. I didn't arrange anything. I was surprised when she waylaid me after I'd been for a swim this morning. From my point of view the meeting was accidental. I didn't break any rules deliberately.'

'And the embrace? Was that accidental?' she queried.

'So you saw that, too,' he drawled mockingly. 'Perhaps I should warn you to watch your step again. You'll have me thinking that you're jealous. Would you believe that the embrace was Beatrix's idea? It was her way of showing her appreciation of my willingness to delay the takeover of the gift shops, and work out some other arrangement so that

161

she can retain control over them.'

As once before Lee was confused by his honesty. He had not denied that the embrace had taken place. He had just skilfully shifted the responsibility for it on to Beatrix, and having met the woman Lee didn't find it hard to believe she would show her appreciation in such a way; especially to an old friend who had been more than a friend in the past, and who would probably be more than a friend in the future.

'Oh, how like you,' she fumed, 'to shift the blame for the meeting on to me and then to blame Beatrix for everything else that happened, just so that you can appear to be in the right. You're the most infuriating, devious man I've ever met and I . . . I hate you!'

Turning, she hurried away from him along the winding rocky passage towards the next cave, puzzled by her own muddled feelings. *Was* she jealous as he had suggested? Jealous of his friendship with Beatrix? But jealousy presupposed love, that she loved him. Not just a little love, but a fierce all-demanding love. Was that what was wrong with her? Had the little love she had felt for him at the beginning of the week, the love a child might give to a close relative who had been kind, begun to grow?

No, no, it couldn't. It mustn't. Hadn't she just told him she hated him? *I hate and love. You may ask why I do. I do not know, but I feel it and am in torment.* She had read those words by a Latin poet somewhere and had wondered at them. Now understanding came to her in an underground passage on a Caribbean island. She hated and loved the man she had married, and the result was torment.

On their return to the hotel she went with Max and Beatrix went with Tiede. Max drove fast along the narrow road. Clouds of dust churned up by the wheels hung about the windows, a yellow haze shot with sunlight.

It was hot in the car, a dry choking heat, and they were

162

both silent. Staring out at the dust, Lee knew that communication between them was at its lowest ebb in the three weeks they had known each other.

How silly Max must think she was, shouting at him like that, telling him she hated him. How childish and temperamental she must seem to a man who had business problems such as takeover bids to think about. He must be fed up with her and wish he could be rid of her.

Tears welled up and ran down her cheeks so that she kept her face turned away from him hoping he could not hear her surreptitious sniffs. He could not be rid of her until his father died, and she did not want Vincent Van Breedan to die because once he had gone her role as Mrs Max Van Breedan would come to an end, a divorce would be arranged, and she would be packed off back to Amsterdam.

When they reached the hotel Max dropped her off and went to return the hired car. She went straight up to her room. In the bathroom she bathed her face and applied more make-up than usual. Wanting something to do to take her mind off the new problems which had reared up that morning, she began to take clothing out of the closet in preparation for packing. There would not be enough room in her cases for the new clothing, which meant that another case would have to be bought.

There was a light knock on the communicating door and at once her stomach muscles crawled with tension. The door opened and Max came in. His face looked a little pale, she thought, but was otherwise impassive.

'Aunt Bertha phoned soon after I left for the caves,' he said coolly. 'She left a message asking me to call her back. I've just done so. She says my father died in his sleep this morning. We'll have to return to Curaçao this afternoon.'

CHAPTER SEVEN

'LEE! It's great to see you again. I've been thinking about you a lot the last few days, ever since you had to leave Aruba in such a rush. Why don't we have coffee together and catch up on all the news? That is, if you've the time.'

The voice was Beatrix's, deep and husky, warm and friendly. She was there, smartly dressed as ever in tailored navy blue with touches of white, the waves of her gilt-coloured hair crisp and perfect, looking businesslike yet feminine.

'That would be nice,' said Lee politely, wishing secretly that they hadn't met. They had both been passing through the traffic-less shopping mall where she had once drunk beer with Max at a sidewalk café and had agreed to marry him.

'You look a little tired and pale,' said Beatrix as they sat down at a table under a blue and white striped umbrella, 'but I'm not surprised. The death of the old man, the arrangements for the funeral and everything must have been quite a strain for you. For Max too. He's been un-attainable.' Beatrix smiled as she fitted a cigarette into a long amber holder and lit it with a gold-plated lighter. 'I know he has, because I've tried to get in touch with him several times about arrangements concerning the gift shops.'

'Yes, it's been very hectic,' agreed Lee, taking off her white sunhat and pushing her hair back behind her shoulders. 'So many relatives came for the funeral. They've all gone now, and Max has flown to Sint Maarten to open the new store there.'

'And you didn't go with him?' Beatrix raised surprised eyebrows.

'No. We thought it best if I stayed with Juliana.'

'Juliana?' Beatrix frowned.

'Yes, you know her. She's Bruno's daughter. Max is her guardian now.'

Beatrix was silent for a moment. When she wasn't smiling she looked hard, thought Lee, and had a mean, downward turn to her mouth.

'I didn't know about that,' said Beatrix slowly. 'You must find her a nuisance, in the way.'

'What do you mean?' demanded Lee quickly. 'In the way of what?'

'Oh, I was just thinking it's a pity she's in the way of you going to Sint Maarten with Max. It could have been an extension of your honeymoon. You'd have enjoyed the trip. It's very different from Curaçao, much more lush.'

'Yes, I expect I would, but Max and I thought it best if I stayed with Julie while she was settling into school. Aunt Bertha has gone away to have a holiday with friends, and Julie still needs a lot of moral support.'

'But you seem so young to be playing the part of mother to a teenager who isn't many years younger than you are.'

'I don't try to be a mother,' said Lee with a gurgle of laughter. 'Julie and I are friends. It all began when I offered to teach her how to play the guitar.'

'I didn't know you could play. In an amateurish sort of way, I suppose?' Beatrix sounded just a little patronising.

'No, professionally. I was playing with a folk-song group in Amsterdam before I came out here.' Lee stopped abruptly, realising she had almost given herself away to this bland woman who had a knack of getting people to confide in her.

The waiter came with the coffee and she hoped that when he had gone the conversation would open on another subject. Her hope was in vain, for Beatrix was too sharp to let such a slip of the tongue pass without comment.

'You were saying you were playing with a group in Amsterdam,' she said as she stirred sugar into her coffee. 'I was under the impression you and Max met in England.'

'We did. It was afterwards that I went to Holland,' muttered Lee, trapped into telling a lie and unable to control the betraying rise of colour to her cheeks.

'How very interesting,' drawled Beatrix. 'That young man, the one who worked for the company when Bruno was alive, he came from Amsterdam last September. I met him one night when Bruno invited me to dinner at the town house. He liked music too, and kept Juliana fascinated while he talked about the Holland Festival and the clubs he used to visit. There was one in particular—I think he said it was called The Golden Tulip—aha! I can see by your face it was the one where you played.' Beatrix was laughing. 'What a coincidence!'

'Yes, it is,' Lee gulped at her coffee. It was too hot and scalded her mouth and throat.

'I've seen him again, you know,' said Beatrix casually, leaning back in her chair and looking about the shopping mall at the people passing through.

'Who?' asked Lee, trying to feign innocence.

'That young man, Adrian. I saw him in a restaurant. He's a waiter there; quite a comedown after the position he had with the Van Breedan company. I wonder why Max sacked him?'

Lee didn't reply, but tried to finish her coffee so that she could make an excuse to leave.

'And how is dear Max?' went on Beatrix, skilfully changing the subject. 'Has he recovered from the shock of his father's death yet?'

How was Max? It was a good question, thought Lee ruefully. How could she tell how he was, since he gave her no sign of how he felt about anything, and communication between them had been kept to the minimum and had concerned only household arrangements and Juliana's future? The breakdown of their relationship hadn't mattered when the house had been full of relatives, nor now that he was away in Sint Maarten. But when he came back, what then? Alone together in the big house except for Juliana, it was going to be noticeable.

The beginning of the end of their marriage, that was the only way Lee could regard his withdrawal from her, and she was sure now that he had known how close to death his father had been when he had proposed to her. Soon he would be suggesting a way in which the marriage could be dissolved so that he could marry Beatrix.

'I don't think it was much of a shock,' she said. 'He'd been expecting it to happen for some time.'

'So Irene told me, when I went to see her in Aruba. She also said that it was the imminence of his father's death which pushed Max into marrying in such a hurry. He wanted to please the old man. Is it true?'

Troubled by this probe, which came so close to the heart of the matter, Lee searched for an answer. To tell Beatrix the truth would be to betray Max's trust, and yet wasn't it in his interests that Beatrix should know the truth and realise there was still hope?

'My dear,' the husky voice was soft and concerned, 'now I've upset you, so I won't press you to answer. When I saw you and Max for the first time in the hotel in Aruba, I thought that my mother had made a mistake and that Irene was wrong, that it was a love-match. I swallowed my chagrin and wished you happy. But later on, once or twice, I wondered. You went so pale when I mentioned Adrian that evening we met, and just now you were disturbed when I mentioned him. You came here from Holland to find him, possibly to marry him. Am I not right?'

Lee nodded miserably. It was as impossible to conceal the truth from Beatrix as it was to conceal it from Max. They were both too shrewd and observant, too well trained in business.

'And he wasn't here?' Beatrix queried next.

'I couldn't find him. I had no money and I couldn't get a job.'

Lee's voice trailed away as she was suddenly swamped by memories of Max finding her at the Leydens' house and comforting her, of the subsequent proposal of marriage, the quiet sunlit wedding, the serene sunny days at the bungalow when she had learned to sail with him, the flight to Aruba, the passion and laughter of siesta hour in a beautiful room; all the happinesses she had shared with him.

'And Max, for once in his life, decided to play the part of knight errant, and went to your rescue by offering you a job as his wife just to please an old man who was dying.' There was a touch of bitterness in Beatrix's voice now. It was there, too, in the curve of her mouth as she tapped ash into the ash-tray. 'You know, Vincent Van Breedan came between Max and me once before. He was a devious old man who put the Van Breedan Company before everything else in his life. He did his best to ruin my father's business and came very close to doing it, and he couldn't bear the thought that one day a son of his might marry the daughter of Hans Volney.'

'You mean ... you believe that Vincent deliberately trapped Max into making a hasty marriage because he knew you would be free, and he didn't want him to marry you?' exclaimed Lee, her eyes wide.

'Something like that,' said Beatrix. 'He was capable of such long-range planning, and Max, as you must know by now, has always been stubbornly loyal to his father. But to return to you, Lee, what are you going to do now that you know Adrian is here in Willemstad? I assume you loved him, otherwise you wouldn't have come out here. Wouldn't you like to see him?'

For once impulse did not take over. Lee thought about the suggestion and came to a conclusion. To see Adrian would help her: at last she would find out exactly how she felt about him, and once she knew that she would know how she felt about Max.

'Yes, I would,' she said, and Beatrix smiled knowledgeably.

'I thought you might like to. I'll take you to the restaurant where he works. They will have his address, I'm sure.'

They went in Beatrix's little car and the manager of the restaurant gave them Adrian's address, as he only worked in the afternoons and evenings. The place was in the area Lee knew, on the other side of the drawbridge, not far from the private hotel where she had stayed when she had arrived in Willemstad.

The house was old and had been divided into small apartments for renting purposes. Beatrix left Lee at the front door and said she would wait for her.

Alone, Lee went up the wooden steps on to the verandah, opened the screen door and stepped into the hallway. She did not have to go up the stairs to the second floor where Adrian lived because he was coming down the stairs, and the sunlight slanting in from an upper window shone on his fair hair, giving its thickness the linten sheen she remembered. He was dressed in a faded blue shirt and blue jeans, but the leap of delight which she expected to feel at the sight of him did not come. He was just another young man with fair hair and blue eyes. He was nothing special after all.

'Hello, Adrian,' she said, and he stopped on the bottom stair to look at her with puzzlement.

'It's me, Lee Williams,' she added, feeling a stir of anger

169

because he obviously did not remember her. 'Don't you remember?'

He advanced towards her, still staring. Then his glance wavered and flicked round the hallway, as if he were searching for some way of escape.

'*Ja*, I remember,' he said at last. 'You are the English girl I met in Amsterdam last summer. What are you doing here?'

'Oh, Adrian, I came here four weeks ago. I looked for you, but I couldn't find you. I didn't know what to do.' Words came in a flood and her voice rose excitedly. Again he looked round anxiously.

'We can't talk here,' he said carefully. 'Come into this room.'

He opened a door on the right and they went into a small dismal room which was furnished as an office, presumably belonging to the owner of the lodging house.

'Why did you come?' asked Adrian after he had closed the door.

'Didn't you get my letter?' she whispered.

'Which letter? There were some when I first came out here. You wrote a lot. My English, as you know, is not so good. I cannot read it well, even though I speak it a little,' he excused himself with a slight charming smile.

'I wrote just after Christmas telling you I was flying out here, as we arranged before you left Amsterdam,' she explained.

'I did not get it—at least, I do not think so. Too many things were happening to me then. Perhaps I forgot to pick it up from the Post Office,' he said warily. 'But I do not understand. Why have you come here?'

'Last September you said . . .' She swallowed painfully, struggling suddenly with her pride. How galling it was to realise that it was true he had not wanted her to come, and that probably Max had been right; Adrian had been running away from a commitment to her when he had come to Curaçao.

'Last September?' he said, grinning and shrugging his slim shoulders. '*Ja*. We were a little crazy, I guess, you and I, last summer in Amsterdam; all that talk about getting married. I did not think you were serious, and that once I was out of your sight I would be out of your mind.'

'As I was out of yours.' For the first time in her life she knew what it was like to feel bitter.

'*Ja*. Not immediately, you know, but I met other women.' Again he shrugged. 'You know how it is, Lee?' he added with a touch of disarming appeal. 'There are many fish in the sea.'

'And Josita was one of them?' Pride was stiffening her now, so that she was seeing him in a more critical light.

He gave her a sharp, surprised glance.

'How do you know about Josita?'

'I went to the Leydens' house looking for you. Max Van Breedan gave me the address, telling me that was the last place you had lived in.'

'Max Van . . .' He broke off, frowning, chewing his lower lip, and for the first time she noticed a slackness about his face, a weakness around the jaw and mouth, a smallness about the eyes. 'You went to the company, then?' he asked.

'Yes. When you weren't at the airport to meet me, I didn't know what else to do.'

'So you know?' He looked wary again.

'That you were sacked? Yes. I didn't believe at first what he told me about you . . .'

'Good for you,' he put in quickly, smiling at her. 'Whatever it was, it wasn't all true.'

'You didn't tell lies, then? Or try to embezzle company money? Or steal the Leydens' savings?' she asked sharply.

For a moment he looked thoroughly disconcerted, and in that moment she recognised that all Max had ever said

171

about him was true. Then he turned away, to draw with his finger on the dust that lay thick on the desk.

'Max never liked me,' he muttered. 'Even when Bruno was alive he tried to get rid of me. He didn't like anyone who might get in his way, he's always wanted full control of the business. I told that little niece of his she was in his way too.'

'Where? When? What did you tell her?' Lee asked urgently, as a piece missing from a puzzle suddenly appeared to hand.

'In the hospital, after the crash, when she was getting better.' Adrian leaned against the desk and shook his head slowly. 'Poor little girl, I used to feel sorry for her. No one took much notice of her and it seemed in my best interests to be on the right side of the boss's daughter, so I took her out a few times. Then after the accident I visited her. That was before Max gave me the push.'

'And you told her she was in his way,' said Lee slowly as she found the origin of Juliana's dislike of Max.

'Ja. I was trying to make her see how vulnerable she was as the heiress to all Max had ever wanted.'

'But she wasn't! She inherited only what her father left to her in his will. She didn't inherit any shares in the business. Oh, Adrian, how could you say such a thing to her? It was untrue and unkind.'

'What do you know about it?' he challenged, a little uneasily.

'I ... I married Max Van Breedan four weeks ago. He told me.'

He was astounded. His mouth fell open and he groped backwards into a chair and sat down hard on it, as if his legs had gone weak. His blue gaze moved down to her elegant sling-back white sandals and up again over the brown and white close-fitting dress she was wearing.

'You clever, clever girl,' he said at last, with a little laugh.

172

'I would never have thought you could catch someone like Max Van Breedan. Clever, very clever to get him of all people to marry a Cinderella like you.'

'Oh, stop it, stop it!' she cried, putting her hands over her ears. He was horrible. He had only one way of doing things and that was to lie and cheat, and because that was the only way he could deal with life he thought everyone else was the same, on the make, out for what they could get. 'I didn't marry him for money or for position. I married him because you let me down and I was stuck here without any money. He offered marriage to give me some protection.'

'You expect me to believe that?' Adrian jeered, and then shook his head. '*Ach, neen.* That is a tall story, as you say in English. Max Van Breedan hasn't an atom of chivalry in him. I know. I've watched him in action with women. For him they are just *objets d'art*, like he buys for the company's store. Sometimes one will take his fancy for a while and he will have a little game with her. I suppose you played hard to get as you did with me, and he fell for it. Yet I would not have thought a man with his experience could have been tricked as easily as that.'

'I did *not* trick him.' The words rang out furiously. 'And you'd best be careful what you say about him, Adrian.'

'*Ja, ja,* I can see that,' he said hastily, rising to his feet. 'I am sorry. I will not say another word about him.'

Lee stared at him, wondering how she had ever believed she had loved him. One flare of her temper and his opposition to her had collapsed. Max had been right. Adrian was below her weight in a battle of wills.

'I'd better go now,' she muttered, turning towards the door.

'*Neen,* don't go yet. I have something to ask you.' He hurried round her to stand before the door, preventing her from leaving. 'Lee, I have to get out of this place,' he said urgently.

'Why?' she asked shortly.

'I ... I'm in trouble. No, not what you're thinking. I haven't stolen anything again. It's a girl.'

'Again?' She could not help the irony and saw him flush with embarrassment. 'I thought you'd got out once and gone to Maracaibo with Josita.'

He made a face and shrugged his shoulders.

'It didn't work out as I'd hoped. I couldn't get work there and she walked out on me.'

'Where is she now?'

'Heaven knows, I don't. She was no good. She wasn't like you, Lee. She wasn't loyal.' His voice softened cajolingly and he stepped closer to her. Once, if he had stood close like this and had used his voice to wheedle her, she would have had great difficulty in refusing him anything.

'What is wrong with this other girl?' she asked, backing away.

'She wants to marry me, as you did,' he said sheepishly, 'and I'm just not ready for marriage.'

'Where will you go?' Her voice was cold.

'I was thinking of Canada. I have an uncle there.'

'Like the guardian you have here?'

'So I told you a little lie! Vincent Van Breedan wasn't my guardian, but the rest was true, he was a friend of my father's. It just didn't work out the way I hoped. I came too late. The old man was ill, they wouldn't let me see him. Bruno was all right, though. He gave me a job and the run of his house, but always at the company there was that dark devil Max, in the background, watching me. Nothing ever got past his notice.' He paused as a new thought struck him. 'How did you know where to find me?'

She told him about Beatrix, and he frowned.

'*Ja*, I remember her. She was after Bruno, making up to

174

him. But she did not like the girl Julie. Didn't want to be a stepmother, I suppose.'

'But everyone says it's Max she wanted to marry!' she exclaimed.

'Bruno or Max. My impression was that either would do. It was their money she was interested in.' He shrugged his shoulders, shrugging Beatrix away. 'Lee, can you lend me some money, enough for the fare to Montreal? I'd like to go as soon as I can, but I don't have the money to pay for the ticket.'

'I . . . I don't know. I'm not sure if I have enough.'

'You must have. Doesn't Van Breedan give you an allowance?'

'Yes, but . . .'

'Lee, once you liked me, you wouldn't have come out here if you hadn't liked me. I could get you to like me again.' He put his hands on her shoulders and leaned forward to kiss her.

She didn't fight. She stood still and let him kiss her because she wanted to find out if it was all over, if she had really fallen out of love with him. Nothing happened within her. She felt no urge to respond, no surge of joy, and finding no response he raised his head quickly, puzzlement flickering in his eyes.

'You were always cool, but not as cool as this. What is wrong?' he asked.

'I feel cool. Adrian, how much money do you need?'

He told her. It was a little less than she had saved for the fare to Amsterdam.

'Shall I bring it to you here?'

'You mean it? You're really going to give it to me?' His eyes lit up.

'Yes, I'll give it to you. Here?'

'*Neen, neen.*' He was frowning, his wits working quickly. 'Bring it to the airport tomorrow afternoon. I'll get a reservation to Miami on the afternoon flight. Meet me at the entrance to the main departure lounge. Can you do that?'

'Yes, but I must go now. Beatrix is waiting for me. I'll see you tomorrow.'

Beatrix was still there, sitting patiently at the steering wheel of her car, smoking a cigarette.

'How did it go?' she asked, as she turned on the engine and shifted the gear lever.

'He wants to go to Canada,' replied Lee woodenly, looking at the narrow inlet of blue water as they passed over the drawbridge, seeing the distant shapes and masts of the schooners and masts of the floating market.

'Are you going with him?' asked Beatrix casually, and Lee turned to her in surprise.

'I wasn't thinking of it. Why should I go with him?'

'It would be a way of helping Max out of a difficult situation. It would be easier for him to get a divorce if you left him, you know. Now that his father is dead he doesn't have to stay married to you, but being a loyal sort of person he won't make any move to dissolve your marriage until you do. Must he and I go through our lives wanting each other, and not being able to do anything about it?'

Again that touch of bitterness. Lee glanced sideways. Beatrix looked calm but sad. Adrian had said he had the impression that the woman wouldn't have minded which of the Van Breedan brothers she could have, it was the money she was interested in. But then Adrian could only see himself in other people.

It was possible that Max had discussed the situation with Beatrix. Perhaps they had discussed it that morning in Aruba when they had walked together on the beach. It could be the reason why he had been so withdrawn lately; he had been cooling a relationship which had shown a tendency to become passionate until Beatrix appeared on the scene.

The car slowed down in front of the Van Breedan town house. Lee turned to Beatrix once more.

'Thank you. You've been very kind,' she said politely.

'I intended to be, and I hope you're going to be kind to me, my dear,' replied Beatrix with her beaming smile. 'I've one more piece of advice to offer. If you want to pay Max back for all he has done for you, you'll leave while he's away in Sint Maarten. Why not go with Adrian? You came here to marry him, not Max. Now you have found him, and the story can end happily for all of us if you go with him.'

'How did you know I came out here to find him? Who told you? Was it Max? Or Irene?' asked Lee.

'Neither. It was Cora de Palm. When I returned to Willemstad after Eric's death, I went straight to see Max. He wasn't there, but Cora told me he had married quite recently a young woman who, she said, was connected in some way with Adrian Hartog. That was all she knew about you. In Aruba I mentioned his name, noted your reaction to it and put two and two together.' Beatrix smiled. 'Go with him, dear, tomorrow, and make Max happy. Goodbye and good luck.'

Beatrix was very clever, thought Lee miserably, as she let herself into the house. As clever as Max was. She was his equal, the sort of woman Lee had always imagined would be his partner; suave and sophisticated on the outside, tough within. And perhaps she was right, perhaps the best way to show Max she was grateful for helping her when she had found herself in a difficult situation, alone without money in a foreign land, would be to leave him, making it easy for him to get a divorce.

She tussled with the problem for the rest of the day and most of the night. By the next morning she had reached a conclusion. When Max returned home that evening she would be gone, on her way to Amsterdam—not because she wanted to leave him but because she could not bear to stay and watch him and Beatrix together and feel continually that she was in their way.

After seeing Juliana off to school she went to the bank and drew enough money out of the account Max had opened for her to cover the cost of the fare to Amsterdam. Returning to the house, she phoned to the airline to make a reservation for the afternoon flight. Then she packed the clothing she had brought with her in her old suitcase, leaving the clothes Max had bought for her hanging in the closet. She put her guitar in its canvas bag and, taking the money she had won at roulette from the drawer where she kept it, she put it in an envelope and placed it in her handbag ready to give Adrian.

All preparations made, she had a quiet lunch which was served to her by Mevrouw Hendricks, the severe-looking housekeeper. She told the woman she would be going out for the afternoon and would not be back until late. Then she phoned for a taxi, wrote a brief note to Max explaining why she had left, and put it on the dresser in his bedroom.

The taxi came. Fortunately the housekeeper did not appear to answer the door, and so did not see Lee lugging her heavy suitcase and guitar out. On the drive to the airport Lee kept her eyes averted from the pretty coloured buildings which gave Willemstad such unique charm. She kept a damper on all thoughts and feelings too; there would be plenty of time for reminiscence and regrets once she was on the plane.

At the airport she paid off the taxi and carried her case to the door where she had arranged to meet Adrian. He was not there, so she put the case down, rested her guitar against it and prepared to wait for him.

Taxis and cars came and went, letting off passengers who were mostly tourists. The afternoon sun was bright and hot, and the north-east wind blew steadily so that flags snapped and crackled as they flaunted their gay colours

178

against the sky of deep tropical blue.

Lee looked at her watch. It was time for Adrian's flight to take off and he was nowhere to be seen. Perhaps she had been waiting in the wrong place—perhaps he was looking for her inside. Picking up her case, she slung her guitar over her shoulder and walked towards the automatic door.

It slid open as she approached with a flash of reflected light, and she stepped through. Inside the departure lounge she stood uncertainly, searching the crowd for a glimpse of a blond head.

A hand covered her hand which was holding the suitcase. Alarmed, she glanced down at it: it was big and muscular, olive-skinned, flecked with black hairs. A fine gold watch glinted on the wrist just below the cuff of a black shirt.

'Your case looks heavy. Let me carry it,' said a familiar voice.

Lee looked up. Dark glasses hid his eyes. His hair was black and curly, his skin was olive-tinted. His mouth was wide and ironic, and his nostrils flared haughtily. He was the devil, her own particular devil whom she had learned to love.

'Oh! How did you get here?' she gasped.

'By air. I flew in from Sint Maarten fifteen minutes ago. I told you I'd be back today. Where are you going?'

He was angry, furious. She could tell he was because he was gripping her hand tightly, pressing her fingers cruelly into the handle of the case.

'To . . . to . . .' The words wouldn't come.

'To meet Hartog?' he rapped.

Flummoxed by his appearance and his correct guess, she glanced round wildly, half expecting to see Adrian rush up and demand the money she had brought for him.

'No, he isn't here,' said Max jeeringly. 'He's run out on you again, and this time with my help. The plane to Miami is just about to take off.'

179

'But how was he able to pay for the ticket?' she exclaimed.

'I bought it for him,' he answered crisply.

'I don't understand,' she gasped.

'I came across him as I left the airport building. He told me he was waiting for you, and I suggested he went without you. He said that until you arrived he could not pay for the ticket, so I bought it for him, glad to see the back of him.' His lips thinned. 'You didn't really think I'd ever let you go with him, did you, *lieveling*?' he added quietly.

'I wasn't going away with him,' she explained quickly. 'I was only going to give him the money for his fare.'

'Then why do you have this luggage?'

'I'm going to Amsterdam. I've a reservation and I'm going to pick up the ticket now. I drew some money out of the account you opened for me to pay for my ticket, but I can give it back to you now and use the money I was going to give to Adrian instead. It's the money I won at roulette.'

'And why are you going to Amsterdam? I think I've a right to know.' He was ice cold now, his anger under control, although his hand still gripped hers.

'I'm leaving you,' she said baldly.

'Why?'

'To make it easier for you.'

'To do *what*?'

'To get a divorce. Oh, Max, you're hurting me!'

'And you're hurting me,' he said in a low furious voice. 'You were going to leave while I wasn't here. You were going to sneak off while I wasn't looking. Was that the way to treat me? Was it honest?'

'But Beatrix said I should go ... ah!' She cried out because his hand had tightened. Max swung her round and dragged her towards the door. It slid open, the suitcase banged against their legs as they went through. Outside some dark-faced boys who were hanging about giggled at

180

the way Max pulled Lee after him.

'People are watching,' she whispered warningly.

'Who cares?' he retorted, and she knew for a certainty that anger had taken over, making him act without thinking.

'Max, wait, please, my hand. You're crushing it!' she pleaded.

He stopped, took the case from her white squashed fingers, gathered it up in his other hand, and set off again at a sharp walk towards the car park.

Sunlight glittered on the smooth satin surfaces of the roofs of many cars. The noise of jet engines warming up made speech impossible. The grip of his hand on hers was still tight, making escape impossible too. She had to go with him.

They reached the blue car. He put the case down but still held her hand. He found keys, opened the boot, threw the case in, took her guitar and put that in too. The boot was closed.

'Max, I can't go back with you! I must go on that plane. It's the only way.'

He gave her a sharp glance and said curtly,

'Get in the car.'

He opened the door and waited for her to move. Lee stood there defiantly.

'I can't . . .' she began.

He leaned forward and kissed her hard on the mouth.

'Shut up and get in,' he ordered.

Still she defied him, standing straight, head held high. The wind took her hair and blew it sideways. The flounce of her skirt was lifted. The skirt billowed up and out. She tried to control both, and as she did so he pushed her down on to the car seat. She moved her feet and legs only just in time to prevent them from being trapped by the door as he swung it shut.

Soon they were out on the road, turning north.

181

'Where are we going?' Lee quavered.

'To the *landhuis*.'

'But what about ...'

'I told you to shut up! Anything you have to say can wait until I've had my say and I'm not talking until we get there.'

'I was only going to say the house is closed up. Don't you remember? You gave Emma and Luiz a holiday,' she retorted huffily.

'That's why I'm taking you there. We'll go to the bungalow where we can discuss this situation in peace and quiet without any interruptions from anyone, including your friend Beatrix Deering.'

'She isn't my friend,' she flared, 'she's yours.'

'I'm not going to argue about that here, so shut up.'

She relapsed into a seething silence and watched the familiar arid landscape pass by. After a while her anger simmered down and she discovered she was glad she had been stopped from going to Amsterdam; glad she was being whisked off into the country by the dark enigmatic man at her side, who had a right to do with her as he liked.

At last the cone of the mountain poked up, glowing pink against the blue sky, and the car dipped down under the tunnel of tamarind trees. The old house loomed up on the right, its windows oblongs of glittering gold as they reflected the westering sun. Under the wheels the stones crunched as the car wound its way down to the bungalow.

In the silence which followed the stopping of the car engine, the only sounds were the washing of the water against the pale sand and the rustle of the wind in the few palm trees. Max got out of the car and walked over to the bungalow. After a few minutes Lee followed him. Where else could she go?

The living room was full of glowing sunset light and the

other rooms were already dim with blue shadows. Max had taken off his sunglasses and removed his jacket and tie. He looked tough and formidable, and suddenly nervous and shy of him, Lee turned and fled into the kitchen. There she searched for coffee and food, behaving in a wifely way, providing sustenance for her husband.

'Leave that.' Her hand was grasped again, and she was hauled into the living room and pushed down on to the chesterfield. Standing solidly before her, arms folded across his chest, head tipped forward, he stared at her from under frowning strangely-peaked eyebrows.

'What's all this nonsense Beatrix has been feeding you?' he rapped.

'She ... she took me to find Adrian. Then she said it would be easier for you if I left you,' she muttered. 'Max ... I know about you and Beatrix. Sophy Volney told me. And Tiede did too.'

'What did they say?'

'Sophy said that you and Beatrix were once inseparable. Even your father agreed that you and she were very friendly before you went to Europe.'

'I'm not denying it,' he replied curtly, 'we did see a lot of each other for a while. I'm not denying either that I found her attractive and enjoyed her company. Beatrix is and has always been clever and witty. But it was all over for me before I ever went to Europe.'

'But Tiede said more. He said everyone expected you and Beatrix to get married, that you were like Romeo and Juliet, and if it hadn't been for parental interference, your father's I suppose, you and Beatrix would have been married ten years ago,' she said.

His eyebrows went up in surprise, his mouth twitched with amusement, and then he put back his head and laughed heartily.

'Romeo and Juliet? Beatrix and I? Never,' he scoffed.

'Although it could have been made to look like that by Beatrix's parents. But it wasn't so. I went to Europe because I wanted to go, not because Vincent asked me to go. He just provided an opportunity and I grasped it.' He frowned and eyed her narrowly. 'Don't tell me you believe all that nonsense?'

'It hasn't been hard to believe it. When Beatrix showed up in Aruba you showed you preferred her company to mine. It didn't take me long to realise I was in the way. She was free at last, but you couldn't marry her because you were married to me,' she said in a small voice.

'So that was why you asked me if I was regretting having married you when we were in the cave,' he drawled, as if something which had puzzled him was at last becoming clear.

'Yes. You'd made it very clear you didn't want me any more, and ... and ...' Lee's voice quivered a little with remembered pain. 'And since we've been back in Willemstad you've ignored me,' she continued shakily. 'In spite of what you said in the cave, you're sorry you married me.'

Head bowed, she watched her fingers twining round each other, thinking she had never felt more abject in her life. She heard his breath hiss sharply in an exasperated sigh and looked up in time to see him swing away to the window to look out at the sun-flamed sky.

'I am not and I never have been sorry I married you,' he said in a hard tight voice, as if he were speaking through gritted teeth. 'How often do I have to say it for you to believe me?'

'How can I believe you when your behaviour since Beatrix came back belies what you say?' Lee countered shakily, and was immediately alarmed because he growled out an oath and banged a clenched fist against the window.

'Think!' he rasped. 'Think back to that night in Aruba when Beatrix turned up. Remember what you said when I

184

asked you if you were still looking for Hartog? You admitted that you were and I felt as if you'd pulled a rug out from under my feet. You see, I was beginning to believe that I might make you forget him. So it hurt when you said that. It hurt so damned much I didn't know what to do, except leave you alone again. When you asked if we could return to Willemstad I assumed you were going to find him. Beyond that point I didn't dare look. But when I saw him today and he told me he was meeting you, I knew I had to get rid of him and risk you hating me again.'

Understanding came to Lee in a flash. She stared at his bulky shoulders, silhouetted against the fast-fading orange light. She had hurt him, and as always when he was hurt he had withdrawn into himself, covering up the hurt with cool, unemotional behaviour, as he had learned to do when a boy. And she had mistakenly seen his withdrawal as regret for having married her.

'Oh, I didn't mean to hurt you,' she blurted. 'I didn't know I had. It was true I did want to see Adrian again, but only to find out how I felt about him. I thought you were still in love with Beatrix, and that's why I was leaving today, Max, to get out of the way, and not because I wanted to leave you. I was only trying to help you.'

'Why?' He swung round again and strode back to her. Sitting down beside her, he took hold of her shoulders and gave her a sharp shake. 'Tell me why you were going to do such a damned foolish thing!'

'Because ... oh ... because I love you, not just a little because you've been kind to me and I'm grateful, but a lot because you're you and you're ...'

'The most infuriating, devious man you've ever met,' he murmured, with a little gasp of laughter as his arms slipped round her. 'I was beginning to think you'd never tell me, *lieveling*.'

She put her hands against him to push him away a little

185

so that she could see his face in the increasing gloom.

'Tell you what?' she asked.

'That you love me. It was most important that you tell me first. I had to be sure you loved me before I dared admit I love you.'

'But why? I don't understand.'

'I've never loved anyone before. . . not like this. I never wanted to marry anyone, until one day a young woman walked into my office. You'll remember saying once that love doesn't wait to be invited?'

'Yes, I remember,' she said softly.

'I found out what you meant that same day. Love came uninvited to me. It was the reason I found myself doing all kinds of uncharacteristic acts, like chasing off to the Leydens' house when I heard that you'd fainted there. I could have easily let you be handed over to the authorities to be deported, but I couldn't because I coveted you. I wanted you to be mine. I wanted to keep you, take care of you, possess you.'

His voice had softened and deepened. She felt his lips brush against tender skin at her temple and she turned her head quickly so that her lips touched his, and for a while there was silence save for their quickened breathing as they kissed with a savage intensity, like lovers who have been separated for a long, long time.

'Why didn't you tell me when you asked me to marry you?' Lee asked, when the kiss was over and she was lying back against his warmth.

'You wouldn't have believed me if I had. You were hurt, on the defensive because of the way Hartog had let you down. You even blamed me a little for that! If I'd told you that I'd fallen in love with you at first sight you'd have either accused me of making a pass at you, which you did when I was in the middle of asking you to marry me, or you'd have accused me of being crazy. I had to find other means of getting you to marry me. I remembered my father's wild threat, and I used it. Your inability to find a job and your innate generosity did the rest.'

'I'd no idea,' she whispered. The room was dark now.

'I had to go slowly, wait for you to recover from disillusionment, but love is patient. I wasn't able to tell you, so I tried to show you in many ways, and that afternoon in Aruba I was sure you understood at last.'

'I think I did, because it was then I realised why I'd been uncomfortable when I was alone with you. I wanted to be your real wife, not just a makeshift one. I wanted you to behave as a husband does in a real marriage, especially when on his honeymoon,' she murmured shyly.

'And there was I being careful, afraid I might frighten you away if I talked of loving you. I was waiting for you to love me before giving any sign.' His scorn was for himself. 'I'm not going to be careful any more, *lieveling*, and you'll have no more doubts about the normality of our marriage in future. Nor will anyone else.'

And as they kissed again in the dark room joy and passion flared up together, so that for a long time there was no more talk; just the muted sounds of two people loving each other freely and without interruption.

In 1976 we introduced the first 100 Harlequin Collections—a selection of titles chosen from our best sellers of the past 20 years. This series, a trip down memory lane, proved how great romantic fiction can be timeless and appealing from generation to generation. The theme of love and romance is eternal, and, when placed in the hands of talented, creative, authors whose true gift lies in their ability to write from the heart, the stories reach a special level of brilliance that the passage of time cannot dim. Like a treasured heirloom, an antique of superb craftsmanship, a beautiful gift from someone loved—these stories too, have a special significance that transcends the ordinary. **$1.25 each novel**

Here are your 1978
Harlequin Collection Editions...

Original Harlequin Romance numbers in brackets

ORDER FORM
Harlequin Reader Service

In U.S.A.
MPO Box 707
Niagara Falls, N.Y. 14302

In Canada
649 Ontario St.,
Stratford, Ontario, N5A 6W2

Please send me the following Harlequin Collection novels. I am enclosing my check or money order for $1.25 for each novel ordered, plus 25¢ to cover postage and handling.

☐ 102	☐ 115	☐ 128	☐ 140
☐ 103	☐ 116	☐ 129	☐ 141
☐ 104	☐ 117	☐ 130	☐ 142
☐ 105	☐ 118	☐ 131	☐ 143
☐ 106	☐ 119	☐ 132	☐ 144
☐ 107	☐ 120	☐ 133	☐ 145
☐ 108	☐ 121	☐ 134	☐ 146
☐ 109	☐ 122	☐ 135	☐ 147
☐ 110	☐ 123	☐ 136	☐ 148
☐ 111	☐ 124	☐ 137	☐ 149
☐ 112	☐ 125	☐ 138	☐ 150
☐ 113	☐ 126	☐ 139	☐ 151
☐ 114	☐ 127		

Number of novels checked @
$1.25 each = $ _____

N.Y. and N.J. residents add
appropriate sales tax $ _____

Postage and handling $ .25

TOTAL $ _____

NAME _____
             (Please Print)
ADDRESS _____

CITY _____

STATE/PROV. _____

ZIP/POSTAL CODE _____

ABC ROM 2228

What readers say about Harlequin Romances

"Your books are the best I have ever found."
P.B.,* Bellevue, Washington

"I enjoy them more and more
with each passing year."
J.L., Spurlockville, West Virginia

"No matter how full and happy life might be,
it is an enchantment to sit
and read your novels."
D.K., Willowdale, Ontario

"I firmly believe that Harlequin Romances
are perfect for anyone who wants to read
a good romance."
C.R., Akron, Ohio

*Names available on request